Finale

Also From Skye Warren

North Security Trilogy & more North brothers
Overture
Concerto
Sonata
Audition
Diamond in the Rough
Silver Lining
Gold Mine
Finale

Endgame Trilogy & more books in Tanglewood
The Pawn
The Knight
The Castle
The King
The Queen
Escort
Survival of the Richest
The Evolution of Man
Mating Theory
The Bishop

For a complete listing of Skye Warren books, visit
www.skyewarren.com/books

Finale

A North Security Novella

By Skye Warren

1001 DARK NIGHTS
PRESS

Finale
A North Security Novella
By Skye Warren

1001 Dark Nights
Copyright 2021 Skye Warren
ISBN: 978-1-951812-44-7

Foreword: Copyright 2014 M. J. Rose

Published by 1001 Dark Nights Press, an imprint of Evil Eye Concepts,
Incorporated

Sign up for the 1001 Dark Nights Newsletter
and be entered to win a Tiffany Key necklace.

There's a contest every month!

Go to www.1001DarkNights.com to subscribe.

**As a bonus, all subscribers can download
FIVE FREE exclusive books!**

Dedication

To Toby, my dog and companion for fourteen years, who passed away this year. He was the sentry over my child's crib. I will miss you forever.

One Thousand and One Dark Nights

Once upon a time, in the future…

*I was a student fascinated with stories and learning.
I studied philosophy, poetry, history, the occult, and
the art and science of love and magic. I had a vast
library at my father's home and collected thousands
of volumes of fantastic tales.*

*I learned all about ancient races and bygone
times. About myths and legends and dreams of all
people through the millennium. And the more I read
the stronger my imagination grew until I discovered
that I was able to travel into the stories… to actually
become part of them.*

*I wish I could say that I listened to my teacher
and respected my gift, as I ought to have. If I had, I
would not be telling you this tale now.
But I was foolhardy and confused, showing off
with bravery.*

*One afternoon, curious about the myth of the
Arabian Nights, I traveled back to ancient Persia to
see for myself if it was true that every day Shahryar
(Persian: شهریار, "king") married a new virgin, and then
sent yesterday's wife to be beheaded. It was written
and I had read that by the time he met Scheherazade,
the vizier's daughter, he'd killed one thousand
women.*

*Something went wrong with my efforts. I arrived
in the midst of the story and somehow exchanged
places with Scheherazade – a phenomena that had
never occurred before and that still to this day, I
cannot explain.*

*Now I am trapped in that ancient past. I have
taken on Scheherazade's life and the only way I can
protect myself and stay alive is to do what she did to
protect herself and stay alive.*

*Every night the King calls for me and listens as I spin tales.
And when the evening ends and dawn breaks, I stop at a
point that leaves him breathless and yearning for more.
And so the King spares my life for one more day, so that
he might hear the rest of my dark tale.*

*As soon as I finish a story... I begin a new
one... like the one that you, dear reader, have before you now.*

Chapter One

Isabella

Most people know me as the heiress to the Bradley family hotels.

It's both right and wrong. I'm my father's first child. His oldest daughter. I stand to inherit most of the business, but I've also been running it since I turned twenty-three.

That's the year we almost went bankrupt.

My father loves travel. He loves it enough to purchase every gorgeous, quirky boutique hotel he finds, regardless of whether it's profitable. And my brother... well, my brother Robin loves being right. He loves it enough to fire every business analyst who disagrees with him.

Between the two of them, they ran the business into the red.

"We don't need him," my brother mutters. Him meaning Francisco Castille, the exiled Duke of Linares. A very rich man who we very much need.

"It's a meeting," I say, smoothing things over. That's my job in the family. Smoothing things over and making the numbers add up so they turn black.

"I'm looking forward to shaking his hand," my father says. "Those villas he built in Bali are sublime. The sheets. The views. And the food. If we could partner with him and get that chef into one of our hotels—"

My brother snorts. "He's not going to give us his Michelin starred chef."

Dad starts to argue. If I'm not careful he'll trade away the entire hotel chain just to get that chef. I put up a hand to silence the argument. "We'll keep an open mind, okay? We'll present our proposal and see what he says."

Castille is known for being a sharp businessman. He's also a recluse, and if the rumors are to be believed, dangerous. After a long and successful run with the bank, the economy turned. No one wants to give money to a hotel right now. And we need money. After our loan request got rejected, we received a phone call from Castille's people. How did he find out? No idea. My brother balked at the idea. My father was curious about it. I'm the one running the forecasts into the next six months, into the next year, and I know how badly we need this. Our receptionist, a woman named Molly who's been working for the hotel since she started as a maid forty years ago, gives us a slight nod. It means he's on his way up.

There's only a single elevator that comes to the top floor.

"Too fucking eager," my brother mutters.

We're standing in a row, waiting to receive him. "We're just being respectful," I whisper.

"Castille would be fucking lucky to sign a deal with us." That's my brother. Always boastful.

"He's royalty," Dad says with a gentle laugh. He's met kings and queens over his decades in the hospitality industry. An exiled Spanish duke does not faze him. It's another day in the life of Harris Bradley. "You know how they love pomp and circumstance."

A discreet ding heralds the glide of the elevator doors.

It's worth its weight in gold, that elevator. The smoothest pneumatic elevator on the market.

Rose marble inside. Titanium doors open, revealing a man.

One man.

I expect an entourage. I expect a security detail. At the very least, a secretary. Instead he's alone. Dark hair. Dark eyes. A strong jaw. That much I knew already from blurry photos from paparazzi. What they could not capture in stolen moments is the intensity that radiates from his gaze. He sweeps us with a look that seems to take everything in—my father's bespoke suit, my brother's brand name clothes. My plain black pantsuit.

His gaze lingers on me. I probably look very different from the blurry paparazzi photos of me during my party girl days. Or maybe I look so different he doesn't even recognize me. With my blonde hair in a tight bun and glasses on my nose, I've been mistaken for the concierge service by more than one hotel resident. I'm always polite. Always deferent.

Now I raise my chin. "Mr. Castille," I say. "A pleasure."

The corner of his lips quirk. "Miss Bradley. The pleasure is mine."

So he does recognize me. I watch as he greets my father in a congenial manner. Fake, obviously. And my brother, who does the handshake squeeze competition. Castille wins that round. He's clearly comfortable commanding a room. And he's done his homework.

That knowing gaze sweeps across the lobby. I can see the calculations in his eyes—from the onyx sofa made of volcanic rock to the champagne brass light installation. No expense was spared in the creation of our new corporate building.

That's part of the reason we're in this mess.

"Exquisite," Castille says in a cultured tone. It sounds like a compliment. My father takes it that way, preening. This is pride and joy. Unfortunately I suspect that it's not really a compliment. Beautiful? Yes. But no hotelier should favor the staff over the guests.

"We were surprised to get your call," my brother says, his tone goading. I tense. "I suppose there's only so far that new construction can get you in this business. Bradley Hotels has all the connections, all the infrastructure."

Castille manages a benign smile. Can't my brother see the powerful mind working behind that calm expression? I want to warn him, but we're on the stage now. This is a performance, this meeting. Every word scripted. Every movement matters.

"Naturally we're very proud of what we've built," my father says.

"Come into the office," I say, moving so they'll have to follow me. We need to get this conversation out of the foyer. Even though it's private here—we trust Molly implicitly after all this time—no deals are signed in a hallway. I glance back and find Castille's gaze on my ass. Heat rises in my cheeks. He's definitely not the first man who's ever checked me out. After my party scene years I almost became immune to it, but I wasn't expecting it here. Not with my father and brother a few steps behind him. Not with a billion-dollar deal on the table.

We settle around the table. My father sits in the center, directly across from Castille. They're the main actors in this play. My brother and I sit on either side.

"About your proposal," Castille says. "I read it. I reject it."

My father laughs, unfazed, though I feel my brother stiffen on the other side of him. "Now, those are just starting terms. Brainstorming, if you will. I want to hear your ideas. Your work in Bali was incredible. If we can bring some of that talent into the Bradley umbrella—"

"Forget it," my brother says, standing. "We're the gorilla in the room. We could make a deal with anyone; we shouldn't even be taking a meeting with this guy."

This is going down the drain faster than I thought. "Let's just listen to him."

My brother gives me a derisive look. "Go back to your spreadsheets."

"The spreadsheets in the proposal?" Castille raises a dark brow at me. "You made those? They were well done. I appreciate a good spreadsheet."

There's no reason the word spreadsheet should sound suggestive, but the way the word rolls off his tongue makes it sound explicit. It occurs to me that I'm the only one at the table with a padfolio. The contract is printed inside, along with other important numbers from our business. Things we'd have to discuss if talks got serious. Castille notices, too.

"Perhaps Miss Bradley and I could conduct this meeting by ourselves."

My father laughs. It's a real laugh, which makes it worse. "Oh, Isa loves spreadsheets. She's always trying to show them to me. There's a time and a place. A time and a place, but we're here to talk about ideas. Now that chef you have at the villas, where did you—"

My brother's still standing. He wants to storm out, but he knows we won't follow him. "I'm next in line to be CEO. If you want to talk about the future of Bradley Hotels, I'm the one you conduct a meeting with."

"I don't think so," Castille says, his voice steel beneath velvet. "My inside line on this company says that the daughter's the one who makes the decisions around here. I'd rather deal with one person than three." He gives a bland smile to my father. "But I'll pass your compliments along to Chef Bautista. He'll be happy to know he has a fan."

Silence frosts the room, and I suck in a breath. Three years ago my mother called me to "do something" with my college degree. We were on the brink of bankruptcy. I spent every night dropping thousands of dollars in Los Angeles. Of course men would offer to buy me drinks. They'd buy me the entire club if I wanted them to, but I always turned them down. Not even a shot. Money makes people think that they own you. One drink leads to another, and then the man expects to escort you home. No, I paid for my own drinks. And when my family needed help, I dropped everything to make it work. A huge loan that we paid back ahead of schedule. Tightening of the budget across all the hotels. And the hardest part, higher standards of luxury and comfort even as we spent less.

No one has ever acknowledged what I do in the company. The average person probably remembers my stunt base jumping off the Hollywood sign. I'm the celebrity punch line.

America's pretty little capitalist princess.

No one cared that I graduated magna cum laude from Harvard.

No one knows that I spend twelve hours a day working.

Except apparently Francisco Castille.

My brother explodes. "Your inside line? Inside line? Does that mean you have a spy here? I need a name. A goddamn name before you walk out that door."

"It's the way things are done," my father says, chiding, relaxed in his chair. A nuclear bomb could go off on the conference table, and he'd take it in stride. It's part of what's made him so successful. It's also what's brought his company to the brink of collapse. He winks at Castille. "Business would be boring without a little corporate espionage. We have someone on the inside of Castille Enterprises, of course. You never know when it will come in handy."

"We don't," I say to Castille.

"I'll speak to Isabella alone." He nods his head toward my father. "And I'll throw in Chef Bautista. If he wants to relocate, he'll have his choice of Bradley Hotels. It will be a condition of any arrangement that she and I conclude."

My brother tries to protest, but my father ushers him out of the room. He gives me one last look before he closes the door—and I read the instructions plain and clear: make the deal. He wants that chef, and he's willing to do anything to get it. Castille clearly understood that.

Quiet descends on the room. It's different from the cold shock earlier. This is contemplative.

Castille leans back in his five-thousand-dollar corporate conference table chair.

I slant him an unamused look. "What's that going to cost us?"

"The chef? I'll throw him in for free."

"Not when you paid a fortune to put his six kids through college, you're not."

"So you do have spies. I'm impressed."

"If you want to be impressed, let's discuss Bradley Hotels. My brother may like to boast, but he's not wrong about our connections. Or our infrastructure. You know that or you wouldn't have asked for this meeting."

"I also know that infrastructure costs a fortune to maintain. That's why you need me."

"Why did you reject our proposal?"

"It's wishful thinking."

"Our numbers are stronger than ever. Cash flow is the problem here."

"And I'm ready to write a check, Miss Bradley. I look forward to a long and fruitful"—he pauses as if tasting the word—"partnership between our families. It won't look anything like what you had written down, clever though it was."

"Clever? No. I think it was fair."

He stands, and my heart thumps. Is he leaving? He can't leave. Except he doesn't head toward the door. Instead he walks leisurely around the table. "Would I see a return on my investment? Probably. If your brother and your father don't run the hotels into the ground. There's only so much you can do chasing after them, cleaning up their mess."

My throat feels tight. It's not only the words he's saying. It's the way he's prowling closer to me. That's what it feels like—as if I'm being hunted. "A return on your investment is good."

"Not good enough. I want more."

Then he's standing in front of me. His body blocks the light from a wall of windows. He becomes shadow—heat and scent. He's intimidating, but I'm not afraid. Instead excitement runs through my veins. An excitement I haven't felt in years. "What do you want?"

Chapter Two

Francisco

The first time I ever saw Isabella Bradley was beneath the strobe lights of my club in Vegas. She looked gorgeous. No, that's not the right word. She looked fuckable. Immensely fuckable, and I seriously contemplated taking the steps down to the floor. She had turned down every man who approached her, but I felt confident enough about getting her into bed. The problem was, I didn't want a carbon copy of every beautiful girl. I didn't want another bland night of vanilla sex. I wanted control, and this girl, with her high heels and fake eyelashes and glasses of Dom Perignon was in no position to give it to me.

What do you want? she asks. The same thing I wanted that night, only now I know that it's possible. It's within my grasp, and the anticipation makes me hard. Everything about her makes me hard. *I want to own you.* If I told her that she'd go running for the hills. "I have something deeper in mind than an infusion of cash."

"You want a seat on the board?"

"God no. I want controlling interest."

Her eyes widen. "That's impossible. Bradley Hotels stay in the Bradley family."

"That's exactly what I'm proposing," I say, drawing out the last word. Proposing. This isn't how I imagined proposing marriage. "That I become part of the Bradley family."

Her blue eyes are narrow. She's suspicious. Good. She should be. "Meaning?"

"Marriage is the easiest way, I should think. And it's about time I settled down. Produce an heir, as my aunt would say."

Shock. Disbelief. Fury. They're written across her face in rapid succession. "You're an asshole."

That makes me laugh. It's a good laugh. A belly laugh. The kind that's genuine. She's perfect for me. Her brother was right when he said I liked new construction. The villas in Bali. The club in Vegas. The ice hotel in Sweden. I like to control every single aspect of a situation. I would never have considered taking on the Bradley hotels, no matter the return on investment. Not until I heard the whispers about her taking over the reins. Not until I put her together with the fuckable woman I saw in the club. The Bradley Hotel empire is a bonus. *She's* my true acquisition.

This close, I can feel her body heat. I can smell her lavender scent. I breathe in deep. It's going to make me hard now, anywhere I go. A lavender candle. An air freshener. My cock will turn to steel because it wants inside this woman.

"Is that a yes?" I ask.

Her blue eyes flash. "There's no way in hell."

"Not even for Chef Bautista?"

"Not for any chef in the world. I can't even tell if you're joking right now. Or just playing some kind of prank. This is a business transaction."

"Our marriage would be a business transaction."

She laughs, a wild sound. I want her to make that sound with my tongue on her clit. "Let's assume I'm even contemplating this idea. Are you suggesting a marriage in name only?"

"Oh darling. We're going to have sex." I glance down at her. That sweet little black pantsuit that she uses as a shield, as if anything could cover her innate sensuality. Every man who meets with her in this conference room wants to spread her naked on the shining wood table. Myself included. "I suppose a test run is in order. A spreadsheet with numbers that add up."

"What?" Her blue eyes are clouded. She's affected by how close we are. She feels the attraction the same as I do. We're both just animals beneath the pretty trappings, and her instincts warn her body to prepare itself.

Her pale skin turns pink. I want to see where else she's pink. I settle for her mouth.

A light brush of my lips over hers.

And then again.

I knew we'd have chemistry, but I'm still surprised by the heat that streaks through me. The hunger. It demands satisfaction. *Here. Now. More.*

I press harder, showing her how it will be between us. I'm commanding in all areas of my life—business and personal. And definitely sex.

"Should I make a table of your lips? Should I draw a graph of your taste?" I murmur to her, probing deeper, questing with my tongue, searching for that feminine flavor. There she is. She holds herself very still as if she's never been kissed.

Her soft cry sounds almost lost, and then she tentatively kisses me back.

This was only supposed to be a test. For her. For myself. To see if we were compatible, to prove to her that we were. A sense of unassailable rightness propels me forward, until I'm nibbling on her lush bottom lip, biting down so I can hear her high-pitched moan of protest.

I'm not touching her anywhere, only my mouth to hers. My hands are at my side, turned into fists so I don't grab her. She's the one who grabs me. Her little hands pull at my suit jacket, tugging, tugging. The warmth of her body seeps through the wool and linen.

She gasps and pulls away, cheeks flushed. "This is in-in-inappropriate."

I'm gratified by that small stutter, proof that she's affected. Because I'm bloody well affected. I thought I was hard when the elevator doors opened and I got a glimpse of that tight body encased in a sophisticated suit. Now I'm so erect I'm aching.

"If this shocks you, wait until our wedding night."

"We're not getting married."

"Don't fool yourself. I could have your pantsuit off, legs spread wide, my tongue in your pretty little cunt if I wanted. You'd come loud enough that your father would hear it down the hallway."

Her blue eyes are midnight with arousal. "Then why don't you?"

Eager girl. I'm going to enjoy her. "We live in a modern world, but I'm a traditional man. The first time we have sex will be on our wedding night."

She scoffs. It would be more convincing if her pupils weren't dilated. If her breath wasn't coming fast. She's the dictionary definition of aroused. "You're insane."

"And you're lovely. Beautiful. Divine. The first time I saw you, I wanted you."

A roll of her pretty eyes. "I bet you say that at every investor meeting."

That makes me grin. "I didn't fall in love until I found out you'd made the spreadsheets, though. Precise. Smart. You gave me what I wanted before I knew I needed it."

"I should call security. I should have you thrown out of the building."

"You won't."

She skirts the table, putting it between us, using it as a shield. "Sit," she says, her voice imperious. She's used to men who obey her. And for now, I will. She's not mine yet. Not mine to control, to fuck, to play with.

I sit down in a conference chair and lean back, hands behind my head. "Are you ready to discuss the terms of our merger?"

Hands smooth her jacket. She gives a little shake of her head. She's trying to compose herself. As if there's a chance in hell I'm going to write a check and walk away. The black padfolio she brought sits in front of me now. We've switched places. I open it and turn the pages. It's a printout of the proposal she sent me, with her notes scribbled in the margins. Ideas she wants to emphasize. Talking points. A few numbers written down.

My eyebrows go up. "That low? You must be desperate for money."

She glares at me. "I should call my father. Make him negotiate with you."

"He'd sell you to me in a heartbeat. I think you know that."

"Then my brother."

"And watch your precious hotel chain go down in flames. You care too much for that."

"How do you know what I care about?"

"You left Vegas. You left the entire club scene. One minute you're getting photographed in short skirts and diamonds. Then Bradley Hotels almost fails. Everyone knew about that one. And you're wearing suits and running numbers all day. You care."

"A hundred thousand people work for this company."

"Isabella Bradley, a philanthropist. The gossip rags will be disappointed in you."

"I'm not running a charity. I'm running a business. And you're wasting my time."

There's a pen in the padfolio. I pick it up where she's scribbled down a number so low that she's clearly desperate. I write a number five times that large. Enough to get her interest. Then I push it across the table. We're negotiating for more than just the company. Her body. That's what I want, and when I want something, I'll pay anything to get it.

Her eyes widen when she reads it.

Then she puts her head in her hands. "This is a disaster."

I could give her some false platitude about how being married to me won't be that bad. But the truth is it'll be worse than she thinks. "A hundred thousand people will keep their jobs. Your family legacy remains intact. Your mother can remain on the board of the natural science museum. She can continue her generous endowment of the arboretum."

"Why would you even want to marry me?"

"Don't underestimate yourself. Every man on the planet wants to marry you. I'm the one who actually has the balls to propose to you."

Her expression turns sardonic. "This? A proposal? I don't see a ring. And you're certainly not down on one knee."

"My methods are unconventional. You'll find that's true in many areas of my life. But make no mistake—I'm not pulling a prank. I'm dead serious."

There's still disbelief in her eyes. It will take her some time to accept this. Like the stages of grief. She'll go through denial, anger, and bargaining. She's mourning her life as a single woman. "So if I say no to your proposal, there's no hotel deal?"

"You won't say no to my proposal."

"See? This is why we won't suit. I don't like some alpha macho man coming in and telling me what to do. I think for myself, thank you very much."

"I'll keep you so sexed up, so blissed out on orgasms that you won't care that much about how commanding I get. In fact, I think you'll learn to love it."

"I'm not some housewife who cooks and cleans."

"If I wanted a cook or a maid, I'd hire one. I want a wife."

"It sounds like you want a sex slave."

"Work all you want during the day. Manage Bradley Hotels. Manage my restaurants and clubs and hotels. I won't stop you. At night you submit to me."

Her face blazes with heat. Vanilla. At least her past experiences have been vanilla. I guessed it right at the club, but she'll experience the full range of kink with me. And she'll like it. I'll condition her to like it. Praise her when she comes, praise her when she cries.

Pleasure and pain.

"Why are we even talking about this?" She probably means for her tone to be demanding. Instead she sounds breathless.

"This is a negotiation."

"It doesn't feel like one. It feels like you're telling me everything you want."

"That's right. There should be something in it for you. Besides the orgasms. Besides the limitless wealth. Besides the title of duchess. There are women who would like to marry me, you know. I'm considered a good catch in high society."

"Then why don't you marry one of them?"

"Because I want you."

Emotions streak across her clear blue eyes. Confusion. Longing. And finally, resignation. She thinks I'm fucking with her. That she won't be able to save her family's company.

She stands abruptly. The chair rolls away from her, pushed by the force of her movement. "This meeting is over. Our secretary will show you out."

Part of me wants to insist that she understand the truth. Another part of me wants to strip her naked, to reduce her to a quivering woman who begs to come. Patience. I don't have very much, but I'll grant her a little. Very little. "I'll wait for your phone call."

She glares at me. "I'm not calling you. We're never talking again, most likely. Our short acquaintance is now over. And we are never, and I mean *never*, ever getting married."

Chapter Three

Isabella, three months later

Lace itches along my arms. A corset restricts my breathing. Garters dig into my thighs. I'm held together by yards of lace and ribbon and satin.

My father appears at my side. He smiles in that real way that crinkles his eyes. "You look beautiful, Isa. I'm so proud of you."

He means it. This is what makes him proud. Not streamlining Bradley Hotel operations. Not overhauling our financial systems. It's this. Marrying well.

That's what makes him proud.

After Francisco left the building, I ran the numbers again. I called the banks again. I rattled the cage of every investor we know, but no one had that kind of liquid money to invest. And so I made the phone call to Francisco, the one he knew I would have to make.

"Thank you, Daddy." He'll never know what it costs me to say that. To swallow my fear and my pride. I studied comportment alongside my multiplication tables. Not one of the five hundred people in the cathedral will see the abject terror vibrating inside me.

His cufflinks are gold. I gave them to him on his birthday three years ago. I wonder if that's why he wore them today. Or if he wore them because they have the Bradley Hotels logo on them. That's his life. His baby. It's also the reason I'm walking down the aisle in Paris, France, in the country that will be my new home. Francisco owns his own private plane. He travels extensively, but his home is a chateau in the countryside.

"You'll be a good wife to him, won't you?" His expression is odd. Concerned, even.

"Of course," I say.

"Of course," my father repeats, looking relieved. "You've always been a good girl. And he'll be a good husband to you." The last sentence is muttered, almost to himself. As if he's trying to convince himself that it's true.

Someone calls to him—I don't see who—and at that moment my brother appears at his side. He's unrecognizable from the man he was in that meeting. There's no bluster, no fight. "You look beautiful," he says, and then he pitches his voice lower. "Don't do this. You don't have to do this. Not for Bradley Hotels. We'll find another way."

The hairs on the back of my neck stand up. "I'm about to walk down the aisle."

"Don't."

"Why not?" There are a thousand reasons not to back out. My family's reputation, for one. The business I've worked so hard to save. But I find myself leaning closer to my brother.

"I should have stopped this." Guilt darkens his expression. "I shouldn't have been such an asshole in that meeting. I've heard things about this guy, Isa. Crazy things. That he's controlling. That he's a freak. And if I don't try to stop you—"

"You can't stop me. This is done." I give him my most confident smile. Francisco said some things during our private meeting. He used the word submit. *At night you submit to me.* If that's what my brother is afraid of, then it's not important enough to risk the collapse of the company. A hundred thousand jobs. I'll trade my body for a hundred thousand jobs.

Even if a knot of fear is forming at the pit of my gut.

"He might—"

The wedding planner interrupts him. She flits around us like a butterfly, making little tweaks to embroidered gauze over my skirt, the tendrils of blonde hair around my face.

Natalie. Her name is Natalie.

She's murmuring into her headset, so it takes me a moment to realize she's talking to me. "Are you ready?" she says in a whisper-yell.

I give her my serene smile. I learned it from my mother when I was five years old. Practiced it in front of the mirror with Estee Lauder lipstick on my lips. It's not only Bradley Hotels on the line. If we were to fail, my younger brother and sisters would suffer. Robin is old enough to take care of himself, but the rest are still in middle school and high school. "Of course."

Robin nods, defeated. "You look beautiful," he says again, and then he goes to take his place inside the sanctuary. My dad ends his conversation and turns back to me.

Natalie beams at me. "You're the calmest bride I've ever seen."

It's not the first time she's told me that. Cake tastings and flower samples. Every inch of this wedding has been planned and purchased. It's the event of the season.

The lights dim in the alcove, the way they do before the opera.

It's our cue. Electricity moves through the air. It makes the hair on my arms stand up. I hear the muted opening strains of "Canon in D." A door opens, and we emerge into the main hallway. The flower girl goes first. A distant cousin. I've met her twice. Then my bridesmaids. Most of them are family friends. I've known them forever, but we don't hang out. My actual friends, the ones from college or people who work at the shelter—they're in the audience. They warranted an invite, but not this particular honor.

My mother picked out the wedding party. My father picked the venue.

And my new husband commissioned the dress.

"Shall we?" my father asks, his lips curved like we share an inside joke.

What would he say if I told him no?

I barely even know the man at the end of the aisle. Who is he? Who am I? I can't do this. Don't make me. He'd probably say I'm being hysterical.

And anyway, I'm not a child. I know my duty.

My family paid exorbitant sums of money in private schooling so that I could repay them in precisely this way—with an advantageous match.

"Lead the way," I tell him with a wink.

It makes him chuckle. "That's my girl. A Bradley at heart."

We reach the entrance to the cathedral. The powerful organ reverberates through the floor. Every single person—man, woman, and child—stands and turns to face me. It would be so easy to flush. To let my heart pound out of my chest and the blood rush to my face.

Instead I lift my chin. I face them down with a calm expression. *A Bradley at heart.*

Only, I won't be a Bradley for much longer. Fifteen minutes, give or take.

My father steps forward. I grip the sleeve of his tuxedo so tight he must feel it. He must feel my terror, but he doesn't seem to notice. He keeps walking, and so I do the only thing I can—I follow his lead. I float down the long carpet covered in rose petals.

At the end of the aisle, my groom waits for me.

Francisco Castille, the exiled Duke of Linares.

I suppose I should leave the "exiled" part off. It's probably a touchy subject in his family. I wouldn't know. I've never met anyone on the right side of the church. They move in European high society, while my family has been strictly New York City upper crust. This will be a merger of more than two people. It will combine businesses and connections. And, above all, this wedding will save my family's entire world. Our livelihood. Our reputation. And the livelihoods of hundreds of thousands of employees. So if my groom is as controlling as my brother warned, then that's the price I'll pay.

That is the price I've promised to pay.

Francisco wears a tuxedo, naturally.

Some men stand stiffly in them. He looks as if he was born in that tux. As comfortable as I might be in my favorite sweater and worn jeans. It's the royalty in him, I suppose.

Black hair. Thick brows. A stern expression.

So far away. The cathedral has to be huge to fit the guest list. Walking closer is like coming into focus, seeing the brackets around his lips, the small slash in his eyebrow. A scar, perhaps. How did he hurt himself? I have no idea. We're basically strangers.

We reach the end of the aisle.

My father moves my hand into Francisco's grip.

Then we're left alone, two of us standing in a sea of people. About to be married.

"Fancy meeting you here," he murmurs.

Through the delicate satin of my glove, I feel his strength. His heat. It's a comfort, even though I barely know him. I match his dry tone. "I heard someone's getting hitched."

His lips quirk. "A wedding, you say. Nothing too fancy."

This from the man wearing a five-hundred-thousand-dollar watch. Though it might be an ordinary daily wear watch when you're a duke. "I thought about dressing up, but then I thought, nah."

His black eyes are molten. His gaze sweeps over me from head to toe. I have the sense he can pull back all the layers of lace and gauze and see me standing here naked in heels. "You look stunning," he tells me, his voice intense. "Gorgeous. There are no words."

"Is that why you proposed?" The question slips out. My mother sits only ten feet behind me. If she could hear me, she'd be horrified. It's not a proper question, especially not as the priest delivers a sermon in a carrying voice. Something about obeying and honoring.

Francisco doesn't appear shocked by my forwardness. "That's part of the reason. You're a beautiful woman. I desire you. Is the attraction mutual?"

The question is a knot in my throat. What would he do if I said no? Would he put a stop to the marriage? It's a ludicrous idea as we stand in the middle of the ceremony.

Then again, in order to say no I'd have to lie.

He's handsome in the tabloids. Distinguished in photos from ceremonies. He takes my breath away in person. It's more than bone structure or tanned skin. It's charisma. An inherent power that he holds as easily as my hand.

"I see," he murmurs. Apparently my pause was answer enough.

"Would you have called the wedding off if I said no?"

He gives a small shake of his head. We're barely moving our lips, barely moving at all. The people in the pews are too far away to see or hear us. We look like any engaged couple in breathless anticipation. "I want you too much for that. Why? Are you looking for an exit?"

I grant him a demure smile. "You *are* handsome. And rich. And titled. It did make me wonder why you wanted a wife you barely even know."

Arranged marriages are common enough among our friends. They aren't announced that way, but when two wealthy families join together, it's often planned. It's not like they randomly meet on Tinder. But the bride and groom do meet beforehand. They've known each other for years, usually. They can both object early and discreetly if it's clear they won't get along.

This? This doesn't happen.

"I know what I want. That's not going to change."

"Not even if I snore?"

His lips quirk. "Do you?"

"I have no idea. I've never slept with anyone else." As soon as the words are out I wish I could call them back. My cheeks heat. I didn't intend to confess that to him—and certainly not in a church. Then again, maybe he thinks I meant sleeping.

The curiosity in his eyes proves otherwise. "Interesting."

"You didn't ask." It's a little much to assume that a young woman is a virgin in these modern times, but he's technically royalty. If there's been a request for verification of my virginity, my mother would have had the family doctor between my legs before I could blink.

"It wasn't a requirement."

The priest is becoming louder, and I sense that we're getting close to our vows. Close to the moment when the plain gold band slides on to my finger, joining the five-carat diamond that was delivered by armed couriers six weeks ago. "What are the requirements then?"

"Honor and obey me." There's challenge in his eyes. He expects me to balk.

I'm considering it. His lineage may go back centuries, but I live in the twenty-first century. Women expect independence and autonomy. I expect those things, too.

Then again, I can hardly feign surprise. A man who wanted a modern marriage wouldn't approach a woman with an offer that included a dollar amount.

No, I knew he'd be traditional.

And I was groomed to be the perfect society wife.

Francisco's expression turns intent. "You understand what I mean, don't you?"

Do I? I thought so, but I have no time to ask. No voice left.

The priest's voice booms between us. "Francisco Absolon Castille, will you have this woman to be your wife in holy matrimony? Will you comfort her, honor her, and keep her in sickness and in health, as long as you both shall live?"

"I do," he says, loud enough that his voice carries to the rafters.

"And you, Isabella Marie Bradley, will you have this man to be your husband in holy matrimony? Will you honor him, obey him, and keep him in sickness and in health, as long as you both shall live?"

Blood thunders through my veins. This one moment will change my life forever. I will honor him. I will obey him. That's what my family needs, even if my knees feel like jelly under my dress. He waits for me with the patience of the moon. "I do."

Triumph shines in his dark gaze.

The priest says a few more words before pronouncing us man and wife. "You may kiss the bride," he says.

"Marie?" Francisco murmurs. My middle name.

I feel lightheaded. Maybe it's adrenaline. Or maybe it's the corset. Or maybe it's the fact that he touches his knuckles to my chin, lifting my face to his. "My grandmother's name."

His head descends.

My eyes flutter closed. In the darkness, I can pretend that no one else is in the room. There's only empty space—him and me, alone.

His lips brush mine. Heat licks through my body. His mouth glances over mine, again and again. It's not perfunctory, this kiss. Not a form of punctuation or even a command.

It's a conversation, much like the murmured one we had before our vows. He asks questions in this kiss and receives answers. My breath stutters. If the kiss in the boardroom was a greeting, this one is an intimate conversation over candlelight.

Light presses between my eyelids. We're not really alone. Everyone's watching us. Everyone's waiting. It feels like the entire cathedral holds its breath. We should stop. I can hear my mother's voice in the back of my mind. There's probably some arcane etiquette rule for how long a couple can kiss at the altar. Whatever it is, we've already gone over the limit.

Francisco is in no hurry. One hand holds me at my waist, keeping me steady on my heels. The other cradles my jaw. I am both cherished and dominated in this moment. I both honor and obey as he coaxes my lips apart. His tongue presses inside for a small, possessive lick. I gasp, and he relents as if he was waiting for my true acquiescence.

Then he leads me down the aisle. I'm blind to the faces on either side. Somehow I manage a bright smile. It's his arm that supports me all the way down.

Chapter Four

Francisco

A virgin. How the hell did I end up married to a virgin?

"Leave us," I mutter to the wedding planner. She's been hovering around Isabella like a bee to a flower. Doing what, I don't know. My bride looks perfect. A perfect doll that I have had dressed to my exacting specifications. It's proof of my perversity that the idea makes me hot. I can move her arms and legs as if she's made of plastic.

I can dress her. And undress her.

The doll in question circles the small room. We're in a private lounge as we wait for the reception to be ready. The crowd sent us away from the church after the ceremony. A photographer rode with us in the limo, snapping away.

This is the first time we've been alone.

"What happens next?" she says, not quite meeting my eyes.

The wedding ceremony was well attended with five hundred people in the cathedral. The reception will be even larger. Almost eight hundred people are pouring into the Bradley Hotel Paris's ballroom right now. They're wearing their best clothes, their finest jewels. Drinking the best champagne as they wait for us to make our debut. "When everyone's arrived, we'll be formally presented to the room. Then dinner. Dancing."

"Dinner?" she asks in a dry tone. "I haven't even started cooking."

She's funny, my new wife. That's something I didn't know about her. There's a lot I don't know about her. "Chicken, beef, or fish?"

That brown gaze flicks to me and then away. "None of the above. I'm a vegetarian."

My eyebrows raise. "For how long?"

"For forever. I saw a documentary in middle school about the treatment of animals in factories and modern farms, and I just couldn't do it anymore."

"Then why are you serving meat at your reception?"

She gives me a tremulous laugh. "Would you have wanted to eat tofu for dinner?"

"I would have wanted to respect my wife's wishes."

"Well, your wife wishes to make the eight hundred people happy."

"What about her husband? Does she want to make him happy?"

"Him, too."

"Then sit down. You're pacing."

She stops abruptly. Her body is completely still, but the delicate white flowers threaded through her hair continue to quiver. It gives the effect that she's flying, fluttering. Constantly in motion. "This is strange. Right? It's not just me?"

"Are you nervous?"

"Of course."

There's a knot in my stomach. "Are you afraid of me?"

"No," she says, too quickly.

She is. She should be. Obedience. Submission. Extreme kink. Isabella might have researched those things. I hinted at them, after all. But she won't understand fully until she experiences them herself.

That's her new reality with me.

A controlled reality.

None of the emotion or drama that plagued my parents. None of the betrayal. This would be a straightforward arrangement. Painless. For me, anyway. There will be plenty of pain for her. Pleasure, too. I have so many plans for her.

Those plans begin now.

"That couch over there," I say in a voice both casual and firm. There's a smattering of armchairs in the room. I want her on the couch, something large enough to support her elaborate gown.

Isabella looks determined, and a little stoic. There's curiosity in her gaze. That will help. And a willingness to please. That makes my cock hard. She starts to sit, but the long train of her gown gets in the way. I help her tuck it over the back of the sofa, help her sit down off her high heels. It's gentlemanly. Gentlemanly unless you know what's on my mind.

I stand in front of her, and she looks up at me. That pose. Those eyes. God. I want her mouth around my cock, but that will have to wait.

Training takes time. The first thing she needs to know is that obedience is rewarded.

"Spread your legs, my dear wife."

Her eyes go wide. "What?"

"You heard me. I'm going to claim my husbandly rights."

"Now? Here?"

I don't bother responding with words. My silence is answer enough. I wait, my cock like iron, my blood pumping. This is what I've been waiting for. This is what I've been wanting. Part of me wants her to rebel, so I can have the sweet pleasure of punishment. The other part knows how to ride the edge, to push her only slightly past her boundaries, to make her complicit in her own debasement.

She swallows hard. "What if someone comes in? What if the wedding planner comes back?"

"She won't." She was hired for her discretion as much as her skill. There is no chance of her coming back inside. It's clear what I wanted when I ordered her to leave. The wedding planner knew. If there's staff outside, they also know. Only my new wife was naïve enough to think I wouldn't taste what was mine.

Isabella spreads her legs—only a few inches apart. Following my order, technically.

"Wider."

She spreads them farther apart. The skirt rides up, showing off her white stockings and bare thighs. She's not wearing any panties. I already know this because I decided on her entire wardrobe, from the dress to the corset to the embellishments in her hair.

I reach down and palm the inside of her knee. And push. With inexorable command I push her legs open until they're spread wide against the sofa. Her cheeks have turned crimson. So pretty. The expansive white lace covers her pussy from view, but I can feel her. I run my hand over her and find her smooth. Waxed, most likely. She's wet, slightly. Slick enough when I run two fingers through her folds. I think the embarrassment has turned her on.

That bodes well for her.

I pull my fingers through her wetness, back and forth, back and forth. "Some will say I'm an indulgent husband. Buy whatever you want. Go wherever you want. Do whatever you want, but when you're with me, your body is mine. I'll use it at any time in any way I see fit. Do you understand?"

Her mouth opens on a silent gasp. "Yes."

"You don't. Not yet, but you will." I find her clit and tap a little Morse code against it. She squirms on the sofa, and her legs close to a fraction. I pinch the inside of her thigh, and she makes a high-pitched whine of pain. Her legs open wide again. "I'm precise in my commands. Clear in my expectations. And firm if you need to be reprimanded."

"Reprimanded?"

I slide my thumb across her clit. And pinch. "There are rewards as well."

She's breathing hard now, her chest heaving in her bodice, her breasts pushing against the bounds of the lace. "Francisco."

"Frans. You can call me Frans anytime you want, except in the bedroom. Or anytime I'm touching your sweet body. Anytime I'm using you, I'm sir. Understand?"

She nods, and I swat the inside of her thigh.

"Yes, sir," she gasps.

"That's good," I say, my voice low and approving. She's learning fast, but there's still so much more to do. "Now I'm going to make you come. I want you coming so hard there's arousal running down your legs. I want you to feel it, dripping down, cooling on your skin, when we go out there and smile at everyone. I want your nipples hard and tight inside your corset when everyone toasts to you."

Her beautiful blue eyes are glazed with lust. "That's... wrong."

"So much of what I want from you is wrong." Obedience. Structure. Discipline. Those things have no place in a modern marriage. I know this. I don't care. I want her under my thumb in every way, but most especially her clit warm and plump and slick.

Voices trickle in from the closed door. "They can hear us," she gasps.

"You must be very quiet." To emphasize my point I pinch her clit, and a small moan escapes her. I don't really give a fuck if everyone hears her climax. I'm a hard man in most ways. Cold. Unkind, some would say, but I know how to pleasure my wife. I lean close and breathe in. Musk. Sex. Woman. A lick from the bottom of her pussy to the top. She squirms against the couch, and I use both my hands on her thighs to hold her down. Lace threatens to block my access, so I shove it up around her waist. There's so much of it, yards of it. Expensive fabric. The gown cost over half a million dollars. It was commissioned by me.

Now I'm tasting her while she wears it. I slide my tongue between her folds, seeking more of her sweet desire.

"Wait," she says, though her hips say otherwise. They rock against my face, finding pressure against my lips, my chin. It's messy, this meeting. It won't only be her thighs damp with arousal. I'll smell her on me for the entire reception. I'll taste her when I eat the chicken or the tofu or whatever the fuck I'm served. "We shouldn't do this here."

"Where would you prefer?" I ask, pausing. My cock's hard as iron. I'm forcing an even tone, but really I want to fuck her into the carpet. "A bed? Would that suit you?"

"Yes." The word turns into a hiss as I suckle her clit.

"How mundane," I say, pulling back to finger her. One finger. Two. She's tight, and my cock flexes with the knowledge that she'll be a vise around me. "I didn't know I married someone who preferred such an ordinary location. Would you like the missionary position with the lights out, too?"

"You don't know who you married."

The words hang between us. My eyes lock with hers. There's pure truth in her words. A little bit of accusation. She may have accepted the merger between our families, between our lives. Between our bodies, but she's afraid of it, too. "You're right. I don't know you. Yet. I'm going to learn you, every inch of you. I'm going to taste every inch of you, too."

It won't be a hardship. I take another lick of her sex. It's hard to hold back the moan that wants to erupt at her flavor. God, she's delicious. Salty and sweet. There's a hint of lavender, too. It turns me on, thinking of her preparing for this. Shaving her legs and her cunt, knowing that her new husband would see her. Feel her. Fuck her.

I swallow hard. A better man would wait until tonight for this. He would give her a bed, with the missionary position, the lights turned off. A better man never would have trapped her in an arranged marriage. But I'm Francisco Castille, the exiled duke. I drive three fingers into her. It's a stretch. She winces. She'll feel more than her arousal when she smiles and waves at everyone in a few minutes. She'll feel soreness, too.

I pump three fingers in and out, slow and steady, relentless in my pace, while my tongue flutters against her clit. Her breath turns fast. Anxious. Desperate. "Please," she mutters. "Please. Please."

Tears run down her cheeks. I push my cock with the heel of my palm. Not yet. I curl my fingers inside her, finding the spot that makes her jerk. A keening cry fills the room as she comes, her inner muscles clenching around me, liquid sliding down my hand.

"You're beautiful," I tell her, my voice hoarse.

She was a porcelain doll during the ceremony, a photograph from a magazine, a bride any man would covet. Now her cheeks are flushed, her lashes glistening, her chest heaving. She's a goddamn wet dream. And she's mine.

I pull out a silk handkerchief and wipe the tears from her cheeks. Then I swipe it over the swollen flesh between her legs. She flinches, still sensitive from climax.

"Thank you," she says, shaky, breathless.

I don't really know whether she's thanking me for the compliment or the orgasm. Or maybe she's thanking me for the money I'm infusing into her family's business. Unease settles in my stomach. *You don't know who you married.* I don't know the details of her life, what she likes to eat or wear, but I know the essence of her. The core of her. She's good and pure, and nothing that I should have soiled with my touch.

She doesn't know who she married, either.

Chapter Five

Isabella

The reception goes by in a blur of faces and smiles. My nipples feel hard beneath the corset, my skin strangely tight. This is the same dress that I wore during the wedding ceremony, but my body feels different now. It's like I've come awake.

Is that what he wants, then? Submission? Because it wasn't so terrible, if it means Francisco licking me until I come.

But then—*reprimanded.*

I'm precise in my commands. Clear in my expectations. And firm if you need to be reprimanded.

I manage to say the right things—*Thank you so much, you're too kind. Of course you'll be welcome at the chateau.* I don't know if that's true. It's Francisco's home. Not mine. I've never even been there, but my clothes and toiletries are being delivered there while I dance. My books are being moved in boxes while I toss the bouquet. My entire life, delivered.

My feet ache by the time we wave our final goodbyes. Then I'm handed into the back of a stretch limo for the long drive. We could have spent the night in the hotel's presidential suite. Could have had champagne and strawberries and a hot bubble bath waiting for us. It's just a private elevator ride away, but I wasn't consulted about the plans. I worked with Natalie on the ceremony and the reception. We picked out the flowers and the cake and the menu, but everything that came after, that was up to Francisco. And he wanted to return to the chateau.

I'd like to pretend it means something sweet, that he wants to spend our first night as a married couple at home. But part of me wonders if he simply does not want the wedding to inconvenience him more than it should. A single day spent in the city and a seven-figure bill. Oh, and a massive investment in Bradley Hotels. That's all it cost to make Isabella Bradley his wife.

Isabella Castille, now. Tears prick my eyes, but I force them back.

"What's wrong?" he asks from the shadows of the limo.

How does he know anything's wrong? It's too dark to see. "Nothing."

"You miss your family."

I'm worried about them, worried about what my father will buy without me there to stop him every day, worried about what my brother will ruin thinking he knows better. Worrying isn't the same as missing them, though. I could have lived the life of a spoiled socialite forever, perhaps. If my mother hadn't called me back to save the hotels. "It's not that."

"Someone was rude to you. One of the guests."

"No, everyone was lovely." I laugh a little to myself because I was introduced to so many people tonight. I will never be able to remember everyone. Though there is one person that made an impression. Francisco's best man. "Your uncle was especially kind."

"What did you two find to talk about?"

His voice is dry, but it feels like a deceptive calm. The water's surface with tiny ripples running through it. "You, of course," I say lightly. "Actually, he told me all about his farm. He had me laughing when he told me about the silly things the calves do. Including the one who got stuck in an easter basket."

"He loves those little beasts."

"I would have thought your uncle was more…"

"Serious?"

"Intimidating."

He gives a soft laugh. "He's plenty serious. And intimidating when you're a little kid with a penchant for getting into trouble. He purchased the veal farm when I was twelve."

That makes me blink. "Veal farm?"

"Don't worry, my little vegetarian wife. They were supposed to be veal, but once he took over and saw their beady little eyes, he couldn't do it. Changed it into a dairy farm. And after my parents died, he moved us into the house there. He thought it was better for me to have a normal upbringing after… Well, after."

I take a moment to digest this. I knew his parents passed away when he was younger. "So he and your aunt raised you?"

"Yes."

His tone doesn't invite more discussion. The irony is that he knows everything about my family. He now owns a controlling interest in our company, but I know barely anything about them. Except that his uncle saved calves from being eaten.

"If you don't miss your family," he says, "and no one was rude to you, then why are you sad?"

He's perceptive, my new husband. And persistent. I'll have to get used to that. "I guess because I'm... afraid."

"Of me?"

"No. Maybe. I don't know you. Or what this marriage will be like. What my life will be like. Everything's changing, and I don't even know what to expect."

"I've told you what to expect."

I make a scoffing sound. "You've told me that you're controlling in the bedroom."

Specifically, what he said was, *I'll keep you so sexed up, so blissed out on orgasms that you won't care that much about how commanding I get. In fact I think you'll learn to love it.*

And I've looked up far too much about that in the three months since we met. Photos. Videos. Books. They make me feel strange, like my skin is too hot and tight. Aroused, that's what they make me feel, though I'm not admitting that to him. Certainly not admitting it when he's wearing a tux and I'm in a designer wedding gown.

"I also gave you a demonstration," he reminds me.

My cheeks heat, remembering the feel of his tongue between my legs. "That wasn't everything, though. It's what I don't know that scares me."

"You want to make me come."

"No, that's not what I meant." My voice sounds choked. I'm embarrassed and...turned on. Why does the idea of making him come turn me on?

"You want to resent me," he murmurs, as if he sees my internal struggle. "I'm the man who bought you. Forced you into marriage so you can save your family. I'm the villain, and you're the noble princess. There's no hero in this story, so don't wait for someone to save you."

"I'm not," I snap, frustrated that he's mocking me. I'm not a princess. I'm not some noble sacrifice. I'm not some dramatic young woman who doesn't understand real life.

"Then learn how to please your husband."

A prickle of warning runs over my skin. "Meaning what?"

"The same thing I did to you at the hotel. Get on your knees."

It shouldn't be demeaning. It isn't. People perform this act in bedrooms around the world every day, at least that's what I tell myself. And Francisco was on his knees between my legs a few hours ago. He wasn't subservient to me, though. He was in control every second.

As I push aside my skirts and drop my knees to the carpet of the limo, I know that I'm not controlling any part of this. Here in the center of the floor, moonlight washes across my dress. I'm bathed in pale light. This is more than sex; it's service.

It should be humiliating, but it only makes me burn hotter.

Francisco takes my face in his hands and looks down into my eyes. The expression he wears is thoughtful. Almost loving. "I'm not going to be nice," he says. "But you are."

He releases me to undo his pants, and it's only in this moment that I understand what this is going to be. He's huge and hard and slick in the faint moonlight, right at the very tip.

I've never done this before. With the way he is, and the things he wants...

My new husband grips his base in one hand and my chin in the other and pulls me inexorably forward until I'm hovering over him.

"I'm not in a particularly patient mood." He says it gently, but I can tell he means it.

"You've been waiting since before the reception."

"Longer. I've been waiting for this since the moment I saw you."

The words make my blood race. I give his crown a tentative lick, and Francisco hisses. Maybe he was going to be more patient than he planned, but now he takes my head in both hands and holds me still so he can stroke into my mouth.

It's a lot. He's a lot. Too much, perhaps. He fills the available space with his first stroke and stops, his muscles tensed. "Suck," he commands.

I don't have any other choice. It's either that or choke. I struggle with the sheer size of him on my tongue. He tastes clean, and I've never known anything to be so soft and so hard at the same time. So thick it makes my lips stretch around him.

Francisco lets me suck him, lets me swirl my tongue around him, until I get a hint of salty precum and he groans. It's the least restrained sound I've heard him make. Fear shivers through me, but it's not the kind that makes me want to scream and run. It's the kind that makes me want to lean into whatever this is and ride it out.

Good thing, because he's not letting go of me.

And I'm not sure I want him to.

Even when he starts fucking my mouth in earnest.

This is a different animal than sucking him while he keeps his hips still. Hot humiliation wraps around me like a second corset. I'm fighting him a little, but I don't want to—it's just that he's hitting the back of my throat, he's pushing past that point, down so deep that I try to push him away.

It doesn't work, because he doesn't want me to get away. He wants me exactly where I am.

His wanting turns my embarrassment back into lust. It is embarrassing, choking on him, gasping for every breath. My makeup has to be a mess. Tears run down my cheeks from the force of his taking. His using. He was using me before, too. Using my pleasure to his own ends. And now he uses my mouth. It makes me unbearably hot.

He thrusts harder into my mouth. This is so demanding. So defiling. I'm in my wedding dress. My expensive, designer lace wedding dress. My husband's cock fucks mercilessly into my throat. It's my wedding night. I was a princess an hour ago.

Now I don't know what I am.

Francisco stops thrusting but he holds me down harder. Pinning me. I couldn't get away if I tried, and I'm not trying anymore. Just in time for him to come.

Hard. Profusely. I swallow and swallow and swallow because there's nothing else to do. No other way to stay alive. I swallow down the seed of my husband until my eyes water. Then I push away, panting, holding on to his muscular leg for steadiness.

He lifts me easily—my entire body weight along with the million pounds of lace and pearls and diamonds attached to me—and pulls me into his lap. I'm in some other world, a dark, wispy dreamscape as he rights his clothing and settles me against his shoulder. The hum of the limo and the steady movement over the highway pull me into a shallow sleep, the taste of my husband still on my tongue.

Chapter Six

Francisco

The limo glides to a stop in front of the chateau. The driver appears to open the door, and I reach in to help her stand. She still wears the beautiful white dress. She hasn't complained about it once. I have the suspicion that if I dragged her across the French countryside in those three-inch heels, she'd only give me that same mild, complacent smile.

That's what I wanted in a wife. That's what I demand.

So why do I have the impulse to ask her what she really thinks?

"Shall I carry you over the threshold?" I don't wait for a response. Her arms reach up to clasp my neck, as if I might drop her. Instead I toss her into my arms. Despite the exuberance of fabric surrounding her, she's light. I climb the stone steps leading to the wooden doors, which stand open to herald our arrival. When we reach the marble floor, I set her down, lingering with my hands on her waist so she can get her balance.

Her cheeks are pink as she looks back at me. There's a smile fighting to get through. A real smile, and I realize how badly I want it. Then she schools her expression back to calmness. "That was sweet," she says.

I nod to the line of people waiting. "My butler. The housekeeper. You can meet with them tomorrow to discuss your requests."

Her eyes widen. She gives them a small wave. It's the first sign of uncertainty I've seen from her. Apparently Mrs. Bradley did not inform her only daughter that she'd oversee staff. I suppose that comes from living in hotels most of her life. There's a general manager to handle that. "Hello," she says.

There are bows. Curtseys. A chorus of, "Hello, Your Grace."

Her eyebrows raise. "Your Grace?"

"They take after the English customs," I explain, but I'm too impatient to wait. Strung too tight with lust over waiting through the wedding ceremony and reception. Waiting for the months to go by planning the wedding. Always waiting for her.

I could have approached her at the charity gala. Perhaps invited her out for coffee. Possibly I could have had her in bed that night, but I don't lose control. I don't give in to my passions. Everything is regulated, even sex.

A wave of my hand, and Lila appears in front of us. "This is your lady's maid."

"Lila St. Charles," she murmurs, her eyes downcast.

"Pleasure to meet you," my wife says, her tone polite and kind and completely unsuspecting. She doesn't know how close she and Lila will become. Lila is one of my very special employees. Her skills extend beyond cleaning and service.

"She'll assist you with whatever you need," I say. "And prepare you."

Blue eyes snap to meet mine. *Prepare you.* She senses the strangeness of the words. Good. She'll have to learn quickly, since she came to me with no experience.

A virgin. Christ.

"Come," I say, taking her elbow and leading her up the grand staircase. Perhaps if I were a better man I would sit her down in my office and explain how this will go. If I were a better man I would give her an option to walk away before we consummate the marriage.

I'm not a better man.

The door to my room stands open. The furniture is dark and stately.

We continue walking. Her rooms are lighter, white with champagne gold accents. A bath has already been drawn in the clawfoot tub. Water steams, swirling with rose petals. A large bed is in the middle of the room with pale blue silk sheets and a canopy. A round antique table sits to the side, surrounded by matching blue-satin chairs. Light streams in from the window, barely blocked by the translucent white fabric covering them.

Lila trails behind us, her hands behind her back. She's well trained.

My wife is not, but that's part of the fun. I'll enjoy training her.

"Lila will service you now," I tell my wife. "Stand still. Lila, you may undress her."

It's a test, of course.

My wife freezes in the well-lit room, her hands by her side. She wants to push Lila away. She wants to demand that I leave. There are a hundred conflicting desires flitting across her beautiful face. This is beyond some inner boundary of hers. Beyond what she imagined our wedding night would be like. She did not think another person would be in the room.

Little does she know.

"Did you think I wouldn't see you naked?" I inquire softly.

She flinches. "No."

"Or that I'd only come to you at night, when it's dark and you're under the covers?"

A flush stains her cheeks, but she lifts her chin. A queen could not be more imperious than she looks now. Her arms lift away from her body. She might be at a dressmaker's for all the concern she shows. "Lila, you may begin."

Lila works first at her gloves, pulling back the satin to reveal slender forearms. I turn an armchair in front of the fireplace to face Isabella. Then I sit and cross one leg over the other. Patience. Control. Command. No amount of wild lust will consume me.

Isabella keeps her eyes on mine while Lila moves behind her. The process of deconstructing the dress happens in stages. The wedding gown comes away first, lifted carefully over Isabella's head and laid over one of the satin-backed chairs to wait. Then her petticoat comes away. It gave her gown its dreamlike shape for our ceremony.

Next comes her delicately embroidered corset.

My bride's cheeks pink up at the loss of the corset, but she doesn't look away. Neither do I. I'm marking time by the rise and fall of her chest.

"Stop," I say.

Lila's hands drop to her sides, her eyes going to the floor. "Come closer."

Isabella glances at Lila, then takes a few tentative steps toward me. Watching her move in the corset and nothing else briefly tests my commitment to patience.

I gesture to Lila to continue. Her hands are efficient on the laces, and my bride stays straight-backed and blushing as the material comes away from her skin to reveal her breasts. Pink nipples. Creamy skin that will mark beautifully. I could tie her hands behind her back and hurt them now, but that's not for our wedding night.

She's starting to wonder when I'll touch her, my perfect bride. I can see it in her eyes. She's remembering my mouth between her spread thighs, hidden from her by the lace of her dress. There's nothing to hide her from me now.

Another test. For her, and for me. A less-disciplined woman might not be able to stand the wait. Might disobey me and climb onto my lap before I've commanded it.

Isabella doesn't. She stands before me in only her heels. A tremble in her arms suggests that she would very much like to cover herself. I wish she would so I could punish her now instead of waiting. It's a powerful wish, and one I won't indulge. She's not ready. My cock disagrees. I overrule.

"Bathe her," I say, gesturing to the steaming tub. "There's lavender oil. Use it over every inch of her skin. Then dry her well."

It's torture to watch Lila's clever hands working over my wife's slippery skin. It's an exercise in restraint, which is of course the entire point. Proving to myself that I can wait.

When the bath is done, the maid dries Isabella with a plush white towel.

I rise from my chair and put a hand on her elbow. My bride allows herself to be guided to the bed. At the edge, she hesitates. Her teeth worry at her bottom lip. The serene expression she wore as she came down the aisle slips back into place.

Isabella does not ask the question I know she wants to ask.

"On the bed," I tell her. "On your back."

Her cheeks turn a deeper red, and I wonder how long she can hold out before she finally blurts out her burning question: *Is the maid going to watch us consummate our marriage?*

No. She will not.

However, what comes next will probably shock her more.

Isabella's knees spread under the pressure of my palms. She keeps her hands flat on the comforter. I run my fingers over her slick folds. Her arousal is obvious and intoxicating. More intoxicating than it has any right to be. I keep my mind on the task at hand. "You're wet," I comment. "But not ready. Lila."

Lila steps forward without hesitation and kneels between Isabella's knees. Isabella pushes herself up on her elbows. "What is this?" Fear sings in her voice, but her curiosity hasn't gone away. She does not close her legs. "Sir."

It sounds so pretty on her lips. "On your back. Lila is going to prepare you for me." I use the same words intentionally. This is the way my bride will learn the shape of my expectations. The range. "Knees wide. Get her ready, Lila. Dripping."

There's a battle on Isabella's face. Her breathing quickens and hitches as Lila puts a hand on each of her thighs and leans in close. "Wait," she says.

Lila pauses.

"Yes, my dear wife?" I ask, my tone mild.

"She's not… you."

I stroke my wife's beautiful blonde hair back from her cheek. "No, she's not me. I tasted you once tonight, and though you were delicious, now your maid is going to prepare you for me. She's going to make you wet and slick for my cock."

My wife flushes hard. "I don't know what to think."

"You don't have to think. Only feel. Are you going to be a good girl for me?"

A short, hesitant nod.

I glance at Lila to give her permission to continue.

At the first stroke of her pink tongue, Isabella closes her eyes.

I pinch one of her nipples. Hard. Her eyes fly open. "I want to see you."

More than that. Lila's tongue on Isabella's flesh sends lightning strikes of need to scorch the earth of my mind. Of emotions. Isabella makes a soft sound, her thighs trembling, because Lila has given up her tentative licks and pressed her face into Isabella's slit. She devours her in hungry strokes, the slip and slide of her tongue loud in the quiet room.

Another moan from Isabella. Her hips move up off the bed, and a small piece of my restraint snaps. "Enough."

Lila pulls away and stands, her eyes on the floor, her hands behind her back. Her chin is coated with my wife's juices. Isabella looks from me to her and back again, lips parted and desperate.

"Leave us," I mutter to Lila, and she exits the room gracefully and silently.

It takes everything in my body and in my soul not to leap over Isabella like a wild animal. The urge is there, and strong. I won't indulge it, or the sharp jealousy that pierces my chest. I wanted to embarrass my pretty bride, and I did. I wanted to push her toward one of her boundaries, and I did. I might also have pushed us toward one of my own.

Between Isabella's knees, I use my hips to stop her from closing her legs and unzip my pants. It's a visceral relief. I've needed this since I touched her after our ceremony. Since I kissed her in front of all those people in the church. Since her mouth was on me in the car.

I thought that would sate me, but I'm aching for her.

"I'm going to take you now." My fist is wrapped tight around my length, and I bring the head to her opening with great care. "There will be pain. You will bleed."

Isabella searches my face, panting. "And you'll—like that?"

"Yes." I'm not going to lie to her.

She's tight. Her opening grips me at first touch. Isabella inches her thighs apart, her expression determined. Her hands close tight on the bedspread. I sink in another inch.

Isabella arches. I can see the pain in her eyes. The shake in her thighs gives away how much I'm stretching her. An experimental thrust makes her breathe out hard. Giving in to the pain. Mastering it, if only a little.

I don't let that happen.

I put my hands on her hips and drive myself in to the hilt, tearing through her virginity with all my pent-up want. Isabella cries out, her cunt clenching. She's mine now. She's been mine since I met her across the boardroom, but she didn't know it yet. Her blood streaks my cock when I pull back, stains the insides of her thighs. I loosen my grip on control. Let myself stroke into her in the rhythm that my body wants.

It's the same rhythm her body needs. I'm intending to circle her clit with my thumb. Intending to force her to orgasm around the pain.

But Isabella does it herself.

Her fluttering muscles coordinate around my cock, pulsing and pulsing, and her blue eyes stay on mine as she comes. It's such an exquisite mix of pleasure and pain that as soon as it's over I drag another one out of her as I reach the crest of my own release. Isabella's tight cunt milks me through her second orgasm, and mine rushes out to meet her. She hisses at the heat, at the way I've buried myself deep to paint her womb with my seed. I am half over her now, and her lips are mine to take, so I take them. A shuddering kiss. Isabella is the one shaking underneath me.

She needs more.

I drag my tip through the hot spill inside her, but I don't pull all the way out. I make her come again with my body taking up space in hers. Claiming it. If nothing else, my bride will understand this—I will take everything, every inch.

After a long moment, Isabella's eyes close. Heavily. Against her will.

With a clenched jaw I lift her into the bed and tuck her in. There is so much more I want to take from her. So much more I want to give her. Pleasure and pain. But the wanting feels perilously close to the fevered emotions that ruined my parents.

I do not indulge it.

My wife sleeps through my leaving. I can't fall asleep for hours. She's everything I could have imagined in a wife. More. The problem is how much I love it. How much I'm coming to crave it. Memories of screaming and throwing things and photographers flashing cameras on the lawn haunt me. I wanted us to have a calm, orderly, mutually beneficial arrangement.

Emotion has no place in a marriage.

Chapter Seven

Isabella

Last night had to be a crazy dream.

There's no other explanation for my lady's maid with her head between my legs and her tongue moving over parts of me that only my husband is supposed to touch—til death do us part. People have strange dreams after big events. Once I read that weddings rank in the top ten of a person's most stressful life events. It makes a certain kind of comforting sense.

But everything else about my new room is exactly how I remember. Blue silk sheets skim my bare skin. Translucent curtains stir over the windows. The canopy drapes gracefully over the posts of my bed. Antique furniture waits for me to sit and what?

I don't know. Tend to my wifely duties, I suppose.

Embroider something, perhaps.

The door to my room opens, and Lila comes in. Her smile is pleasant and professional. I could almost imagine last night never happened except for the knowing glint in her eyes.

My stomach twists. It was real.

Last night happened. Oh my god, last night happened.

I sit up and pin the sheets to my chest.

"Good morning, Your Grace." Lila doesn't appear bothered by the fact that I'm still abed and covering myself with the sheets. She glides into the bathroom and returns a moment later with a silk robe that matches my room—white, champagne accents, a pale blue lining. Lila adjusts it over my shoulders like she's done this every day of her life. "What would you like for breakfast? An omelet? Blueberry pancakes?

Pain au chocolat? His grace has already shared with us that you do not eat meat, but we have many other options."

"Oh, I couldn't eat," I manage to say.

She gives me a small smile. "Chef has been up since three a.m. baking. He wants to impress you. He's a very emotional cook, so unless you want ratatouille every day for a week, I suggest you order a large breakfast and send back your compliments to the chef."

"Yes," I say promptly. "I'm ravenous. Please prepare a sideboard in the breakfast room."

A small wink.

I'm stunned at how Lila moves us swiftly into my new morning routines without a hint of embarrassment. Everything she does is experienced and professional.

I try to match her energy. That's what I was born to do. Bred to do.

To marry well, and be a good wife to my husband. To let Lila fuss with my hair and bring me clothes from the enormous walk-in closet and lick me between my legs until I'm a soaked, writhing mess if that's what my husband tells me to do…

God.

I stand up from the chair at the vanity in my sparkling dressing room, cheeks burning. "I'll go down for breakfast in a moment," I announce, as if I'm calmly organizing my day instead of freaking out inside. "First I'm going to speak with my husband."

"Yes, Your Grace," she says, hesitating for the first time since we met.

My cheeks heat. "If you could point me in the right direction."

"Please follow me," she says, sounding relieved. Of course I have no idea where to find my husband. Before last night I never stepped foot in this house.

After an hour-long hike through plush carpet and marble and gleaming wood floors in a herringbone pattern, I'm shown in to my husband.

Francisco is working in his study. It's a large, masculine space with miles of worn leather paneling. It feels like a throne room, and Francisco completes the illusion. He sits behind a large, hand-carved desk, a slash of sunlight across his face. The desk is made of Bocote, one of the most expensive woods in the world, with a gorgeous, contrasting grain. Everything about him is as pressed and perfect as he was for our wedding.

He's like this all the time, isn't he? Always in control.

A large gray dog sits at attention next to his desk. His dark eyes narrow on me. He lets out a bark, and Francisco's eyes come up from the sheaf of papers he's been reviewing. There's frank possession in his gaze...and a light there, too. He's pleased to see me. I try to be less pleased to see him. Try to keep my guard up. There are things I need to discuss with him before this goes any further.

"This is Isabella," he tells the dog as casually as if it's human. "My wife."

Every time he calls me that, another shock of disbelief and pleasure runs down my spine. I like how it sounds. But I don't like this unmoored feeling I have. The marriage to Francisco was supposed to be advantageous for my family and his. It was supposed to be simple.

The maid's face between my legs does not seem simple.

The dog's ears perk up as if he understands his master.

I drop to one knee. "Come here, sweet puppy."

The dog lets out a whine of excitement and comes running up to me, giving me a big, wet lick across my face that has me laughing.

"Down, Wolf," Francisco says.

Wolf completely ignores him and rubs his massive, furry body into my arms. Francisco mutters something about poor training and snaps his fingers. Finally the dog glances at his owner and slinks away to sit by the desk again.

Brushing the gray fur off my clothes, I make my way to the chairs on the other side of Francisco's desk and sit, back straight, chin up. Focus. This is not about the fact that he has an adorable monster of a dog.

"Last night was...unexpected."

"Was it?" he asks, his tone bland.

"I'd like to discuss it. I'd like to discuss what kind of marriage this is, exactly." I keep my voice even and calm despite my very frantic thoughts. Despite the desire and shame and confusion that have all descended on me at the same time.

"The usual kind, I suppose. Though I've never been married before." His dark eyes meet mine. "I did prepare you for what it would be like between us."

"You said you were commanding in the bedroom. That means... what? Giving orders. Following them. Maybe you'd use a flogger. I was prepared for a lot, but not that."

His lips quirk. "You want me to use a flogger?"

"Don't make fun of me."

"I'm not laughing, my dear wife. Though what I actually said was that I'll keep you so sexed up, so blissed out on orgasms that you wouldn't care that much about how commanding I get. I said you'd learn to love it, and I think I've been true to my word."

True to his word? *True to his word?* "Last night. I don't even know what to call it."

"A threesome."

A little charge of electricity runs through me. "Yes. That. You didn't say there'd be threesomes."

"I didn't spell out what we'd do every night. Even I haven't decided that far in advance. I'll give the orders. You know that much; you just don't know what the orders will be."

I'm flushed with both adrenaline and arousal. This is my first fight as a married couple. Neither of us is shouting, but it's a conflict. One that might break us up before we've even made it a week. We'd be slaughtered on Instagram for breaking up so fast. They would crucify me for being a capricious socialite again, but I don't care about that. I care about the investment in Bradley Hotels. That's what's at stake here. "Tell me what you'll order me to do. Describe it in detail, Francisco. That's what I need from you."

He steeples his hands together, considering. There is a very real chance he'll refuse my request. And then where will that leave me? Like Alice falling through the endless blackness, down the rabbit hole of sexual eccentricity. It doesn't help that in these seconds I notice how strong his wrists look. How capable his hands look, hands that knew just how to touch me.

Finally Francisco nods. "All right. I will do my best to describe my plans for you. For us. I want things to be plain. To be clear. The last thing I want is drama in this marriage, in my life."

The last sentence sounds like a warning. "Good," I say with more confidence than I feel.

"I expect you to be a good society wife, to host dinner parties and galas. And because you have an interest and a talent in it, to manage my hospitality investments."

Relief fills me. This part I can handle. "Great."

"And in bed," he proceeds, "I expect you to be sexually subservient."

My breath catches. "Sexually—"

"Subservient, yes. With whatever my requests might be. I'll never ask you to do anything dangerous, but it won't always be comfortable. It will be pleasurable, most of the time. Unless you don't follow my orders well enough. Then there might be corporal punishment."

I'm failing at one of my first and most important qualities—poise. My cheeks must be on fire. I've definitely lost my composure if my face is going up in flames.

Hot embarrassment chokes me like a hand around my throat.

"You misled me." My voice comes out hoarse. I meet Francisco's eyes over the offending paper. My skin is hot enough to scorch it, but I try to keep my breathing in check. "This isn't how the marriage was described to me. You never said anything about corporal punishment."

"What did you think would happen if you disobeyed me?"

"I don't know! Nothing." I'm half up out of my chair. "I'm a grown woman."

"Then why are you shouting and stomping your foot like a toddler throwing a temper tantrum?" Francisco's tone makes me feel small.

"This isn't a tantrum. It's being upset. A grown woman is allowed to be upset." My voice shakes. It's not the voice I should be using in this room, with this man. It's not the voice I expected to be using at all in this new life of mine. But the even tone I've practiced and cultivated and used to my advantage all my life seems as out of reach as the moon.

I'm out of my chair without realizing it, already standing. My emotions jostle one another for prominence, and I hate it. I hate the twist in my stomach and the heat in my face and the desperate sense that I don't know where to look. I feel used and bought and afraid—and that fear makes my knees quake.

"Isabella." The corners of Francisco's mouth turn down.

He is still gorgeous, even when he's frowning. The hint of disapproval in his eyes makes me feel more afraid.

And it makes me feel a twisted desire. He's scolding me. Reminding me that my role is to sit quietly across from him. To honor and obey. Not this. It's not supposed to be this heated.

I don't sit down.

I can't.

"This is too much," I say, backing away. "I can't do it. I didn't agree to this. I'm out."

I have to get away from him and everything in this room. From the gaze that sees everything I'm afraid of and the golden morning sunlight in his hair and the adorable dog. Running from this anointed king is the only way to save myself.

It's futile. I know it as soon as I take the next breath. I won't be the daughter who ruins things for her family. I won't be saving myself, either. There's no way out of this agreement.

I turn on my heel and go. If I can't get out of this marriage, then I'll take the next best thing—getting out of this room, where his eyes can't follow me.

Chapter Eight

Francisco

Wolf whines, wanting to go after her, but I give him a firm no.

I give my dear wife two hours to cool off.

She's right, of course. I should have told her the full extent of my demands in the bedroom. I should have been crystal clear about the way I would take and own and use her body.

I should have outlined, in black and white, what that would mean in practical terms. It means she is never to close her thighs to me. It means she can cry and shake and beg, but she can never walk away. It means I'll order her lady's maid to lick her pretty little pussy until she comes.

Why didn't I tell her those things?

Why didn't I sit her down, look her in the eye, and recite the list?

Probably because I knew it would scare her away. It would terrify a woman like Isabella, already so innocent and cloistered. Even her party days with champagne and dancing didn't prepare her for me. Nothing could have prepared her for me.

There was evidence enough of that in her eyes. All that pretty shock and horrified desire. I would have liked to take her chin in my hand and watch the expressions roll over her face.

Not on the first day.

She needs this time to let her new reality settle in. Of course, she won't leave. Not with the infusion of cash her father is probably already squandering.

Isabella needs time to adjust. She felt pleasure from Lila's attentions last night. The sounds she made testified to it. A little humiliation will go far with her.

Patience is the highest of all virtues in this particular moment. I exercise it for most of the afternoon before I dismiss my staff and go looking for my wife.

It was three years ago when I saw her at the club. Isabella was with her friends, the five of them drawn in a tight circle to dance for a bachelorette party. They took turns fending off guys and replaying their excitement again and again. Isabella played her part to perfection, the way she did for our wedding and for the wedding night.

Her body was utterly tantalizing. Every movement drew me in. The sway of her hips. The fall of her hair. I wanted to know how she looked on her knees. Wanted to see her that way in the middle of a crowd.

My imagination was interrupted at the moment she made a graceful exit.

She gathered up her purse from their booth and moved away from her friends with promises to return quickly and a relieved set to her shoulders.

I waited fifteen minutes before I followed her. An absurdly long time, looking back. Patience was a virtue then, too. Because Isabella was too absorbed in the music to notice me when I finally found her hiding place.

An unused private room. Hard bass vibrated through the room from the main club, but Isabella seemed oblivious. She sat at a piano we kept around from when the club had live music. The song she played was slow and haunting. Lonely. A poignant counterpoint to the frantic copulation of pop music out there. My cock was already hard from the sight of her dancing. The music did something else entirely. A knowing snapped into place. I would have her as my bride. I would do whatever maneuvering it took to make that happen. She would be mine.

Now she is.

I let Wolf out to roam the grounds outside and start my search in the quiet places in the chateau. Isabella is not in her room, or the sitting room, or the library. She is not in her walk-in closet or even mine. I need music. That's where she'll go.

I'm right.

I find her in the ballroom, where a grand piano sits draped in heavy linen when it's not in use. The fabric has been pulled away and neatly folded. It sits beside her on the bench as she plays. It's a different song than the one from the club but just as haunting. She scrambles to her feet when I come in, eyes fiery. "Go away."

"We should talk."

"I don't want to talk to you."

I step farther into the ballroom, crossing the parquet flooring that has been worn by a thousand feet and then shined to faultlessness, worn and shined. "We're going to talk anyway, my dear wife. You'll use your words instead of sharing your feelings with the piano."

"Or else what?" Her blue eyes flash like a stormy sky. A dimple appears in the center of her chin to highlight her determination. "You'll use corporal punishment? You'll spank me?"

My hand itches to do it. Aches to do it. Isabella is the picture of heated frustration. She's pink-cheeked and angry and pushing. These moments are opportunities to demonstrate her role. To demonstrate mine. My wife will not be a whirlwind who flies through the house every time she disagrees with me. She won't refuse to talk to me when she does. I won't have it.

This, despite how hard I am. I never wanted the kind of relationship my parents had. There was too much acid. Too much acrimony. Emotions ran far too high to be controlled or managed. In my own life I insist on control. And I will have it here, too.

"Calm down." I keep my tone level. Isabella won't force me to match her in this. I feel a pull at the center of me that keeps my back straight and my eyes on hers, unwavering.

"So you'll actually spank me." She folds her arms over her chest, and the corner of her mouth turns up. "You'll punish me. Your hand. My ass."

"It's tiresome to repeat myself this often, so I'll say it a final time. If you refuse to discuss this rationally with me, then I'll use other methods to convince you."

A punishment won't change her mind… at first. It's a heightening of the emotions already in play. For the person who is submitting to the punishment, this presents itself as pain that builds to release, followed by clarity. Isabella needs this as much as anyone I've ever seen.

"Well, I won't be calm. Why should I be calm? You lied to me." She stabs a finger in my direction. "You purposely hid things from me so I wouldn't understand. You're a liar. You're an asshole, exactly like my brother said."

That amuses me. "Your brother warned you about me."

"He said people talk about you. That you're controlling. That you're a freak."

"Is that so?" It's oddly endearing to me that he tried to warn his sister. If only her father had been as concerned with her welfare as he was about his hotel.

She lifts her chin. "And he was right."

Isabella's eyes widen as I stalk toward her at the piano. There's fear in those eyes, of course, but other things, too. A quicksilver flash of relief and desire. I cage one hand around the back of her neck and turn her when I'm seated on the stool. Then I bend her over my lap. Isabella struggles within my grip. "You're not doing this. You're not going to do this."

I pause, leaning back enough to let her escape if she really tries. "Do you want me to stop, Isabella? Or should I call you Isa the way your family does? If you really want me to stop, say the words."

"Bastard," she says. Her hips buck unconsciously against my leg. I consider telling her, but I don't want her to notice that she's enjoying it. Not quite yet. "Asshole. Freak."

"And apparently you knew that before you married me, so what are you so shocked about?" I flip her dress up to expose the curve of her ass. Isabella wears no panties, no thong, nothing. She won't be wearing them in my house unless I give her express permission.

That will come later, when she's trained.

Now she's as wild as an unbroken horse, swearing extensively. I'd be impressed if I weren't so irritated. This is not the Isabella I agreed to marry, and now we'll spend valuable time making her into that woman.

"Now you tell me what happens next," I say, still giving her enough room to escape if she chooses. "Am I going to spank you? Or are you going to walk away from our contract?"

She shivers, and I know it's not entirely fear. It's curiosity. Arousal. "I hate you."

That's answer enough. "Every time you speak you earn five more."

The first five swats are hard enough to stun her. Isabella reaches for her ass with one hand with a shocked gasp. I pin her arm behind her back. She had her chance to walk away. She didn't want it. "If you can't keep your hands still, I'll tie them," I inform her. "Trying to cover yourself is a good way to get hurt."

"I'm already hurt."

I cut her off with another series of hard spanks. I had intended to go easy on her for her first punishment, but no. That won't get her attention. "You're hurting in the moment, but there won't be lasting harm. No, you're simply being punished. You disobeyed my commands, and these are the consequences."

This time, I give her ten. By the last one Isabella is panting over my lap and crying out with every contact. I rub a palm over her pink flesh. "That's enough," she breathes. "You did it. You punished me. You spanked me."

I cover her mouth with my free hand. "I love your voice, my dear wife. Except when I've expressly forbidden you from speaking."

Another ten.

It's hurting her more now. Her cries are turning to whimpers interrupted with sharp gasps that make my cock throb. And between Isabella's legs, she's slicking up. I haven't touched her there yet. I don't need to. I can scent her arousal, and it makes me want to bury my face between her legs and lick her until pleasure becomes its own punishment.

Instead I keep spanking her in a relentless rhythm that turns her bottom a darker shade of pink and then a deep red. Isabella lasts longer than I expected before she gives in. It's a subtle thing, with a woman like her. A delicate curving of her body over my lap. Her surrender isn't some big, showy display. It's a tiny surrender in her posture. She stops trying to get up, stops trying to pull her wrist out of my hand, and lays herself over my knees like she should have done all this time.

Five more, and she offers her ass up to my hand.

Isabella's crying now, red-cheeked and quiet. A softer man would stop. Would soothe her burning flesh with his hand and murmur that she had done well. Her punishment has not made me feel particularly soft or gentle. It's made me want more from her.

I take more.

Ten more stinging slaps across her ass, as hard as all the others. Isabella sobs through them, her hips rocking against my leg. When I'm finished, I pull her off my lap and stand her abruptly in the middle of the pantry.

God, she's beautiful like this, with tears on her cheeks and humiliation pink on her cheekbones and her hands stoically at her sides.

"We can discuss it," I offer. "Or I can bend you over my lap again. I'd accept either outcome."

"You weren't honest," she whispers. "Sir."

"No," I admit. "I wasn't. A lie of omission is still a lie, and I omitted plenty."

"That's a terrible apology."

"Probably because I'm not sorry. It made you my wife. If you had run scared, I never would have gotten to fuck you. To spank you. To hold you." There is one more thing I need to do before we leave this ballroom. Isabella wants it. She doesn't know what it is, not yet, but I can see from the trembling knees and the errant tears still sliding down her cheeks that no one has ever needed this ritual, this closure, more than Isabella does now.

I stand up and fold her in my arms.

The tension in her body doesn't last. She sags against my chest and takes big, deep breaths while I rub her back. I do not tell her she's done well, because she fought like a hellcat.

"I'm not sorry," I murmur into her hair. "I want you too badly for that."

Chapter Nine

Isabella

I hope that Francisco might let up a little after the ballroom.

I'm dead wrong. He doesn't back down at all. I'm not sure what I thought he would back down from—being himself? Taking what he wants? No. Not that. A small part of me thinks he'll soften, and we'll playact newlywed bliss.

There is bliss. Not the kind I expected. It confuses me in a way that I didn't expect to feel. I can count on Francisco making me come and writhe underneath his hands and beg. He does it every day, without fail. I just didn't think it would be...like this.

With a man like Francisco, it was impossible not to think he might be dominant. But he's more than dominant. He's royalty, and he rules every room he walks into in this house.

The morning after my spanking he strides into my dressing room and tells Lila to strip off my clothes. She does it without hesitation, and I find myself helping her. It's Francisco who licks me that morning, not Lila, though he does make her stand close enough to see every movement of his tongue. I burn hotter with embarrassment with every hour that goes by. Every hour that he orders me to bend over this item of furniture or that item of furniture and display myself for him.

He's not shy with my body, or with using it. Whenever he wants. Wherever.

Whoever is in the room. It doesn't matter. All that matters is the force of his desire.

It's a powerful thing. I can't stand up to it.

And worse, I don't want to.

A deep-seated voice in my mind reminds me over and over again that this kind of sex pushes the boundaries of propriety. The fact that it makes me so wet mortifies me until I realize that voice is the outside world. A jealous outside world.

A world that wishes a stunning, powerful man would bend it over the arm of a sofa and spank it until it was wet and squirming and crying all at the same time.

It's never going to be simple between us.

I'm always going to have complex feelings about Francisco and the lies he told to get me to marry him. Lies of omission. He was up front with me about his expectations in a broad sense. Never the specifics.

I don't forgive him for that. I *can't* forgive him, can I?

He spanks me for every reminder, as if to drive the point home. Not enough to be a true punishment. Just enough to remind me of the deal we made.

A deal that's very much still in effect.

On the fifth day, I wake up on my back.

It's strange for me. I'm usually curled up on my side or sprawled out over a pillow, but sometimes when I'm dreaming especially hard I'll end up flat on my back. I don't remember the dream. It still feels too early to get up, so I try to turn over.

And I'm stopped by something tugging at my wrist.

Something metal.

I jerk both wrists toward my body. They don't move. They don't go anywhere, and it's only then that I think to open my eyes and find out what the hell is going on.

Francisco and the butler look down at me from the edge of the bed. All my covers have been stripped away, and there are chains. Heavy and strong and with only the slightest amount of slack. I open my mouth to question my husband.

He looks at me from beneath those heavily lashed eyelids, daring me to defy him.

Maybe I would have, in the beginning. Maybe I would have raged and cursed and tried to run. Only two of those things are options for me now. I can't run, and what I feel isn't rage. It's more complicated than that. Hot desire is already pooling between my spread thighs. The cooler air in my bedroom teases me there. I'm getting used to other people in the room, but the butler's presence still makes my face heat and my breath hitch.

His presence and the flogger in his hand.

Not my husband's hand.

The butler's hand. Anthony, that's his name.

He's handsome enough, with dark golden hair and a square jaw. It reminds me of the way household help in Regency England would be chosen for their attractiveness. Is that how Francisco chose him? And more importantly, did he choose him because he found Anthony attractive or because he thought his future wife would?

Francisco smiles down at me, the corners of his mouth curved in a darker cousin of delight. He backs up with deliberate care, creating exactly enough space for the butler to come forward.

"Begin."

At Francisco's command, Anthony brings the flogger down on one of my breasts. The leather tails sting over my swollen nipples. My back bows against the bed. There's nowhere for me to go. Anticipation makes every hair on my body stand up. Somehow it's worse, being able to see it. I thought a blindfold would be the worst thing, but no, it's being able to watch the flogger fly toward me while I am powerless.

Lust flares in Anthony's pale brown eyes, but that's not what turns me on. He's not the master of this scene. He's not Francisco. No, he's merely a prop. A prop like the thin black flogger that plays over my stomach and down over my thighs.

Francisco makes a sound of disapproval, and the butler shifts to the foot of the bed. No. Surely not. That's not what he's going to do, and not what Francisco meant. I fight back the question on my lips and force myself to wait. The few moments it takes him to get to his new position are enough time for me to feel everything.

My mind rebels against the idea of the butler and the flogger and my husband, standing nearby but not wielding it himself. It's wrong for him not to be the one to do this. Isn't it? But as his eyes move possessively over my body, I realize it's not wrong. It's a sign of his power. He commands everyone in this household. He might as well have the flogger in his hand. It's the same. Everything springs from him.

The flogger comes down between my legs.

It sends me spiraling. Francisco wanted this. He wanted to watch the tails of the flogger connect with my softest, most secret flesh. He wanted to watch me cry out and hear that cry turn into a moan. He wanted to watch me thrash against the bed, held in place by chains he put around my wrists and ankles himself. I know he did.

"Three more," he says.

The first one is a shock to the system. All that leather on already sensitive flesh. The second cracks me open. And the third wrenches a sudden orgasm out of me. I'm not the kind of woman who comes from this kind of treatment, except that I am. Except that Francisco made me this way. Or brought it out of me. Maybe these desires were always there, always hiding under the surface. It's possible I was always this filthy and depraved.

This is as bad as it can get. This is as wrong as it can get.

"Fuck her throat," says Francisco.

It sounds so elegant, coming out of his mouth. Almost like a royal edict.

Anthony doesn't hesitate. He climbs up on the bed and straddles me. I'm so completely exposed. So completely at his mercy. I'm at my own butler's mercy, except it's really Francisco's mercy, and Francisco isn't going to be merciful.

The butler unzips his pants and takes his cock out. Francisco hands him a condom the way you'd hand someone a cigarette, and the butler unwraps it and rolls it on.

I open my mouth.

"Good," says Francisco, and a pleased flush moves from my forehead to the tip of my toes. Praise from him shouldn't do this to me. I haven't even been his wife for a month. It makes no difference. It's humiliating. Horribly humiliating, the way this makes me feel. I was not raised to crave compliments in situations like this. I never thought that being a good wife would mean opening my mouth to accept the butler's cock.

I never thought that it would give me a twisted pleasure.

The butler leans over me and pushes in against my tongue. I don't like the taste of the condom, but it makes this different from Francisco. He can enter my mouth without a barrier. Apparently, the butler cannot. Everyone in this house is an extension of Francisco. His word is law. So the butler fucks my mouth like he owns it, too, with deep, almost frantic strokes.

Francisco watches.

Impatience builds in his eyes, and my body matches it. I don't want him to be impatient. I want him to give in to his impatience and touch me. He doesn't do it. Francisco rarely gives in to anything.

"Ten seconds." His voice holds no sign that he's bothered in the slightest by how long the butler is taking with my mouth. For his part, the butler fucks harder. His hips jerk as he spills himself inside the condom. It's hot through the rubber. There's no time for him to enjoy it. He climbs off me, and off the bed, and puts his uniform back into place. The only sign he was just stroking down my throat is the pickup in his breathing. Francisco sends him away with a look.

It's only when the door is closed that my husband removes his clothes. He's perfection in them and breathtaking out of them, all bronzed skin and hard muscles. Naked, it's clear what fills out his tuxedos so beautifully. He has a powerful physicality. Francisco climbs onto the bed without preamble, and now it's not the butler's uniformed thighs straddling me, it's his naked, hair-dusted ones.

Then his crown is between my lips and I'm taking him into my mouth, steel under velvet skin, and I wrap my tongue around him. How do I feel this feverish for him and this suspicious of him at the same time?

Francisco laughs. "You were holding out on our poor butler. Do that with your tongue again." I do, and a low groan escapes him. "I have to fuck you for that."

He has to fuck me, and I have to take it. I'm chained to the bed. Held open for him by lengths of metal. It makes my hips work faster as he positions himself between my thighs and strokes inside me. I'm wet, soaked from the chains and the butler and from Francisco's eyes. He stretches me anyway. My husband fucks me like it's his personal mission to find out how much I can take. I manage his thick length by fucking him back. I let my hips work themselves into the pain instead of away from it, and then the pain goes away. I'm being stretched by him, taken by him, but it doesn't hurt. I clench on him over and over.

Francisco angles his hips so that my clit gets more contact, and this sends me tumbling over and into another orgasm. It tugs on the memory of the flogger, and another release comes hard on the heels of the first one. I'm so dirty. These things we do are wrong. They're wrong for a good wife and a good daughter. I don't say a word of this to Francisco. He'd only fuck harder. Punish harder. Take more.

"One more time on my cock." Francisco reaches between us and finds my clit. It's too sensitive from coming so much, but his finger against it is impossible to ignore. The chains hold me down, but it's his hand that makes me feel caged in by him. It's a painful pleasure at first. Francisco watches my face intently. For signs that it hurts too much?

No. For signs that he should fuck me harder. He does, and it has the outcome he wanted. I come again as he fucks me, taking me with a kind of abandon he'd never show in front of anyone outside this household. He's bared to me in this moment.

I come in a short, jagged burst. That's the last one. No more.

"Why?"

Francisco lifts his head to where he'd rested it against my shoulder. "Why what?"

"Why does it feel so good?" I mean for it to be a joke, but it comes out plaintive, almost sad.

My husband leans down and kisses my bare shoulder. "Because it's what your body wants, my dear wife. You can't deny it. You were made for this. You were made for me."

Chapter Ten

Isabella

The nights pass in a sensual haze. The days take new shape. Reports come to me about the operations and financials of Bradley Hotels. I'm away from day-to-day operations now that I live in France. Even with access to a private plane I'm eight hours away. I can't look over my father's shoulder or manage Robin's temper, but it turns out I don't need to.

"Isa," my father says, his voice pleading. "The hotel is a gem. A hidden gem. There's this window in the private dining room overlooking the Rhine that is absolutely stunning."

"I believe you, Dad. That's not the point. We can visit the hotel all you want, but Bradley Hotels doesn't need to acquire it. We already struggle with the municipal requirements on our properties in Munich and Frankfurt. Another hotel would mean more oversight."

"The legal department can handle that," he says, his tone dismissive.

And they can handle it. While hiring more lawyers specializing in international law, raising our baseline costs, and swallowing into the profit margin of a small hotel. "I'm sorry, but the numbers don't add up." I pause for a moment. "You could invest some of your own money."

When Francisco demanded controlling interest in his contract, that meant he gets the final say in any major deals or decisions. He cedes management to me, which means I get the final decision. It's almost like he purchased Bradley Hotels as a wedding gift for me.

I still deal with my father and Robin, but I have the final say.

My father pauses. The air over the phone feels heavy. "Is this coming from Francisco or you?" he finally asks.

I look out the beveled windowpanes. The angled glass sends through a profusion of color—endless green with pink and blue flowers. Fields of lavender beyond. My office is smaller than Frans's. More delicate. Feminine. It has paintings on the ceiling like his, angels instead of demons. Wolf splits his time between us. Right now he's snoring gently by the white marble fireplace. It would be easy to make Frans the villain in my father's story. But it wouldn't be true. "It's coming from me," I say, my voice gentle but firm. "It would be a bad move for the business. It might not be right away, but we'd be heading for another bailout, another loan. We'd end up laying people off, and how would that help the hotel? Better that we do what we do well. The company is financially stronger than ever now that we have Frans's backing. We need to keep that momentum, not derail it."

"He's changing you." My father's voice sounds small. Petulant.

Maybe he is changing me. Or maybe I'm becoming more myself. I soothe my father's ruffled feathers and end the call. Wolf rests his head on my knee, as if he knows that I'm troubled by the accusation. What if I'm becoming someone else here?

"Problem?" comes a low voice.

My husband stands at the door, his body leaning against the frame. Even though we work from home most days, he wears a suit every day. It fits him as comfortably as another person might wear worn jeans and a threadbare sweater.

"No problem," I say, keeping my voice light. "There was a hotel in Bonn that my father fell in love with, but it doesn't fit into our portfolio."

"I saw the numbers this week. Very impressive."

It's ridiculous that I flush when he compliments my spreadsheets. "Thank you."

"You don't have to do this work, you know. I have managers if you want to step back."

"Oh no. I love the hotels. I mean, maybe someday I'll stop working, once I—" My cheeks heat. *Once I become pregnant.* I don't say the words, but he hears them anyway.

"Once you give me an heir?"

My nose scrunches. "Do you want a boy so badly?"

His expression softens. "A girl would be fine. If she was like you."

When he says things like this I can almost forget that this was an arranged marriage. That this was a financial contract. I'm falling for my own husband. It's a dangerous place to be, because he's clearly holding back. "I'd like a boy, too. If he was like you."

His expression closes. "Right. Someone to carry on the family name."

He turns and departs as abruptly as he arrived. Wolf gives me a guilty look before he abandons me to trot after his master, leaving the room empty and painfully quiet.

Chapter Eleven

Francisco

The weeks that follow are a blissful state of marriage. Better than I could have imagined.

Naturally they come to a terrible, crashing end.

Isabella comes into my office with high color in her cheeks and a frown on her gorgeous face. That's enough to put me on alert. No one in this household should be making her feel this way. No one but me. "Are you busy?" she asks, her voice tight.

"Too busy for you? No."

Isabella turns up the corner of her mouth. It's not a reassured smile. "My dad needs my help."

I arch an eyebrow at her. "Your help?"

"Yes." She looks at her hands in her lap. This is the least composed I've seen her since the day she fled to the ballroom. Isabella might lose control in the bedroom, but rarely elsewhere. "He's gotten into some kind of deal that's gone south."

"The hotels?"

"No, it's another investment. This private jet company he signed with his personal money."

"He wants you to leave your home and your duties here to renege on a deal he signed?" My god. The man seemed nice enough when I dealt with him leading up to the wedding, but he's an incompetent fool. What kind of man has his daughter run to cover his ass? "No. You won't be doing that, Isabella. I forbid it."

She blinks. "You forbid it?"

"I do."

"Who gave you the right?" Isabella's tone has gone sharp enough that I wonder if I'll have to bend her over the desk. But there's nothing playful in her eyes. There's nothing to indicate she would submit. "You don't tell me what to do during the day."

"I absolutely will give you direction if you're running back to your daddy every time he calls."

"It's only been the once." Isabella's eyes come up to meet mine, determined and dark. "He hasn't called me about anything since we've been married."

"In a month. We are still, for all intents and purposes, on our honeymoon. You'll let your father handle whatever mess he's made."

No matter the impression I had of Isabella's father during the wedding planning process, one thing remains true. He's terrible at business. He let his daughter arrange a marriage to save him from ruin. How many times will she run back into the burning building of their hotel empire?

Harris Bradley was a great hotelier. Put him in charge of a boutique hotel; he'd make the guests happy. It's the millions that caught up to him. The billions. He wasn't made to manage that kind of fortune, which is why he squanders it. Isabella's been saving him from himself, but she won't be doing that anymore. He sold away his greatest asset when he gave me her hand in marriage.

Isabella glares at me across the desk. There is no lightness whatsoever in her expression, only a piercing betrayal. "This is insane."

"He doesn't have any discipline," I tell her. "And with no discipline, that makes him unpredictable. It makes losses for his companies inevitable. That kind of man can run through any amount of money if he has the chance."

"*Work all you want during the day*, you said. *Manage Bradley Hotels*, you said. *I won't stop you*."

"This isn't managing a hotel. This is managing your father. And if you leave for the meeting now, you won't be here tonight to submit to me. That was part of the deal."

"I'm going to the meeting." Isabella sits up tall. Very tall. She looks regal in her wrap dress and flat shoes, perched at the edge of one of my office chairs. "And you can't stop me."

"Absolutely not."

"You said that your control would end at the bedroom door. This has nothing to do with our sex life." She blushes when she says this. It's endearing enough to make me forget she's arguing with me. My cock is hard, damn it.

"I know my own terms." I want Isabella under my control. I want her to submit to me like the pretty wife she is, rather than fighting me over her father's business deals. I want her to understand that this is for her, not for me, and that I don't want her precious time and breath wasted on his incompetence. "And the terms make me your husband. You're not running to save him from himself, and that's final."

Her breathing quickens. "You can't be serious."

"I'm absolutely serious. If you need me to bend you over this desk to convince you, then say the word. I'll be happy to show you how very serious I am."

"No," she bursts out. "This is bullshit. And I'm going. The meeting is tomorrow."

Isabella moves to stand, but I stand first. She's shouting at me. She's shouting, and while part of me recognizes that she has every right to do that, the other part of me is a small little boy cowering under a table while his parents throw million-dollar vases at each other across the foyer. I swore I wouldn't have this kind of marriage when I grew up—drama and fighting. Control. I need to maintain control. "You're not racing to your father's rescue every time he calls. The man will clean up his own mess or he'll have to live in it."

Now my wife gets to her feet, pale with anger, her hands balled into fists at her sides. "I am his daughter. He asked me for help. And I'm going. I'm going, and you can't stop me."

"Isabella."

"I want an annulment."

"No fucking way." My heart clenches. What if I pushed her too far?

"I want the whole marriage wiped from history. You wanted control in bed? Fine. You want to tie me up and let your butler flog me in front of you? Fine. Have Lila watch while you punish me? Fine. But you don't get to take my family away." Tears shine in the corners of her eyes. "They're mine. I worked all my life for them, and you're not going to take that away because you have some stupid obsession with pretending to be a king."

Searing emotion works its way through my chest. I'm not the one taking advantage of Isabella to make up for my own helplessness. I was clear with her about our agreement, and her father is being a dishonest, manipulative bastard. He shouldn't be able to reach into my marriage and stir it up, for god's sake.

My jaw aches. This is exactly the situation I'd hoped to avoid. Planned to avoid. I won't let it continue. I won't have a house full of strife and spectacle. "I'm not pretending to be anything, unlike your father. You, on the other hand—"

She richly deserves to be bent over the desk for this. Isabella would like it, in the end. My belt across her ass would bring her thoughts into calmness.

But a bright line has sprung up between us. The line between the bedroom and the rest of the world. An annulment. She asked me for an annulment. I won't cross that line now. "You are not the woman I married. I won't entertain childish temper tantrums in my office."

"And I won't entertain controlling bastards trying to micromanage every minute of my life. I'm not your property, Francisco. You don't own me."

"Thank god for that." There's nothing I loathe more in the world than being at the mercy of emotion, and I'm very nearly there. How was she able to wound me like this? It shouldn't be possible. Not in the life I've built and the person I've become. It feels like I need her, but I can't need her. I can't allow myself that weakness. I force steel into my voice. "You're useless to me this way. I would be embarrassed to have you on my arm."

"Then we're in agreement." Pain stretches Isabella's voice, and regret crashes into me. "Draw up the papers so I can sign. I'll pack my things, and we won't have to see each other again."

"That would certainly be for the best." Another lie.

I want to see Isabella every day. I had intended to make her training process slower, to give her time to adjust to her new life. I haven't been able to do it. Need for her wakes me up in the morning and keeps me up after she's fallen asleep. This morning, I was going to propose a new living arrangement. I thought she might be open to sharing a bedroom, or at least a bed.

Isabella stares at me, her arms tight across her flat stomach now. No telling what she's waiting for. I won't be the one to break. I won't be the one to show her that she's hurt me. This has gone far enough. We've crested the peak of pointless emotion, and I don't see any recovery for it in this conversation. That's not how these arguments work. They fester and spread until taut silence takes over the entire house and everyone in it.

No escape, other than death or divorce.

Or, I suppose, an annulment.

Swallowing the hurt and the attendant sting takes more effort than I would have thought necessary. I've already let myself indulge in this exchange for too long. It ends now. I force my face back into calm detachment and force my heart back into a steady rhythm and keep myself firmly on the other side of the desk. I won't go to her. I won't touch her. Isabella will get what she's requested from this meeting.

"Anything else?" I ask, my voice ice cold.

Isabella blinks, very nearly a flinch, at my tone. It's the same tone I'd use for any member of staff who needed to leave. Her throat moves. I very much want to grip her there and feel the tension and desire in her pulse. My mastery of myself doesn't allow it.

"No." Her voice wavers. "There's nothing else."

I'm distancing myself from her, though we stand in the same room. It's a series of gates coming down between the two of us. Thick, heavy gates, because behind them I'm a bloody heart who doesn't truly have his own balance. That man—that reckless, irrational one—is willing to fold first. He would go around the desk and apologize, take her in his arms, and then take her to bed. No maid. No butler. No artificial distance between us... No one but the two of them.

That man would fall to his knees, tell her he'd fallen in love with her, beg her to stay.

I'm not that man.

"Then you can go. I'll send for you when the papers are finished." I sit at my desk and reach for a pen. The things I need to ask for will be simple enough. Isabella hovers at the edge of my vision, swallowing and swallowing. I fix her with a cold stare. "If there's nothing else—"

Hurt flashes through her eyes. "No. There's nothing else between us."

My wife turns her back on me and goes out of my office without a backward glance.

Chapter Twelve

Isabella

Packing is impossible.

I don't know what to take. None of my old things seem to be available. I search through drawers and find myself unable to pick out any items that weren't bought by Francisco as part of my new wardrobe. It seems unlikely that I only came here with a pair of pants, a top, and two sheath dresses, but everything seems wrong.

Perhaps it's me who is wrong. My head is clouded with anger and the lingering cuts from his words. I thought Francisco wanted me here. I thought he wanted me at all. That was the reason for our arrangement. He chose me. And now he's glad to be done with me.

And I'm glad to be done with him.

I keep repeating this lie over and over while I rifle through my walk-in closet. I don't want to be with him. I don't crave the things he does to me in the bedroom. I don't need to see the lust and want in his eyes every time I enter a room. I can live without hearing the sounds he makes when he lets go during sex. None of that matters.

It shouldn't matter. I toss a cashmere sweater into the brand-new luggage I've found with a frustrated growl.

A soft knock at the door makes me pull up. Snap back into the good wife, though I won't be Francisco's wife for much longer. Lila stands at the threshold, surveying the open suitcase and the clothing tumbled into it. "His Grace sent some paperwork."

"Good," I say, too brightly. "Let me see it."

I keep my jaw set so I don't cry as Lila hands me a leather portfolio. It falls open in my hands. It should be easy enough to read the print on the page, but I can't get past *Agreement to Annul.* My eyes blur. Why? He's giving me what I asked for.

Lila puts a soft hand on my arm. "You're upset. Can I help you?"

"We had a fight," I blurt out. I shouldn't be airing my marriage's dirty laundry to my maid, but what is there to hide from her? She's been between my legs. She sees everything. "My dad asked for help with his business. There was—there was a bad deal he wants me to smooth out. He got in over his head. The meeting... it's happening tomorrow. I'd have to get on a plane right now to make it. Francisco said I couldn't go."

Lila is frowning. "Forgive me if this is too far, but is there a reason your father couldn't negotiate on his own behalf?"

"No. He could do it. He signed the original deal. It's just his way of..."

My maid moves past me to the suitcase. She bends to take the clothing in her hands, then folds each piece and tucks it into the space. "His way of doing business?"

"His way of never having to deal with the consequences." It's so obvious, now that I've said it out loud. This is the same reason I offered myself in marriage to Francisco. Not just because I love my family and want the best for them...but because my father refused to take responsibility. He let me carry it for him, and he wants me to do it again.

Lila stands and pats the front of her uniform. "Francisco believes in responsibility." She presses her lips together, seeming to make a decision. "His own family suffered from a lack of it, though not when it came to business."

My heart aches. "What was it, then?"

"His mother and father, the former Duke and Duchess of Linares, were not a match for each other in terms of their personalities. They both saw each other's weaknesses and exploited them. Emotions ran high. I have to imagine it was stressful for His Grace."

"Not a match. What do you mean?"

"There was fighting, constantly. Screaming." She glances at the door, furtive, as she knows she shouldn't be talking about this. "There was infidelity on both sides. The household, we thought the young duke would never marry. Not after the wreckage they made."

"That's terrible."

"It was how they died. One night after a fight his mother drove away, furious, enraged. There was an accident. His father went after her.

He found her in the moments after the crash. She died in his arms. The former Duke of Linares never recovered from his grief."

My memory of the conversation in Francisco's office is different now.

I see it filtered through my own past, and his. He was quick to see what I couldn't about my father, and of course I didn't want to believe that. He's my dad. That doesn't give him free rein to use me the way he's been doing. Though I will never abandon my family, I also don't need to go running every time they call. After all, my first duty is to my marriage now.

And the way I behaved...

No wonder it made his face close off. No wonder he dismissed me like one of the maids. He witnessed a lifetime of that kind of fighting. Francisco saw it at its most frantic heights.

And its most painful depths.

"I..." I'm about to apologize, but it's not Lila who needs that from me. He didn't handle the situation well; he could have explained. But at least now I understand. He thinks control will help him avoid the fate of his parents. "Thank you. For telling me all this."

She nods and returns to the door. "Send for me if you need me."

When I'm alone, when I've blinked the tears away from my eyes, I read the agreement.

It's not the vengeful document I'd imagined when I threw it in Francisco's face. In fact, it's generous to a fault. My family keeps everything. They keep his investment, his backing. They even keep the damn Michelin-starred chef from Bali. They won't have reason to blame me for ending the marriage. And, in its last paragraph, it releases me entirely from any and all agreements that Francisco and I have entered into. Without consequence. There's even a provision for support lasting a full year after the annulment is confirmed.

He cares for me.

Enough to put aside the things I said to him and have this delivered to me. This—a door back to my old life, if I want it, and offered without spite or malice. This portfolio is freedom, from our marriage and from him.

I don't want it.

My heart beats fast and hard at the knowledge, pumping blood into my cheeks and making the tips of my fingertips tingle. I don't want it. Because I care about Francisco, too. I've been so busy with my own confusion that I never bothered to learn about him. There's a wild heart beneath all that control and dominance.

I want more of his dominance, too. I was a fool when I fought him in his office. He was willing to stand between me and my father's exploitation. It was, like everything with Francisco, more complex than what I let myself see. He would have been the one to take the fall for my refusal, not me. He would have done that for me.

The portfolio snaps shut in my hands, and I'm headed for the door before I know where I'm going. Out. Out of my bedroom, out into the hall.

I find the butler on his way from one floor to another. He pauses when he sees me rushing for him, making frantic eye contact. "I need your help."

"Of course, Your Grace."

"My room."

Anthony follows me silently back to the bedroom. My heart flutters up into my throat, but I close the door and face him with my chin up. "The bindings that my husband uses on me. Do you know where he keeps them?"

"I do."

"Get them out, please."

The butler leaves the room, and I try to calm my racing heart. Step one is to remove all my clothing. I fold my dress neatly and put it on one of the blue satin chairs, along with everything else I'm wearing. Then I take the papers out of the portfolio and take them to the fireplace.

It springs to life with the flick of a switch. I'm certain I'm not supposed to burn things in there, but it feels too right. The flames eat through the papers and curl them into ash. I'm watching them burn when the butler returns. His arms are full of leather bindings with hooks and clips meant to anchor them to the bed.

We exchange a look, and I'm almost swept away by a powerful sense of gratitude. Thank god I don't have to explain to this man what I want. Saying the words, even after the time I've spent in this house, would be too much. I go to the bed and lie down, stretching my arms and legs wide, and he moves efficiently around the mattress.

When he's finished, I've been thoroughly bound for my husband's display. I test the bindings. They hold. The butler has done his job well. He looks down at me from the side of the bed, calm professionalism on his face. This is a man who has flogged me and fucked my mouth. It doesn't affect his ability to do his job.

"Is there anything else you needed?"

Part of me wants to ask him to send Francisco to my room, but I don't want that. I deserve to wait for him. Naked and exposed to anyone from the staff who chooses to walk in.

My face flushes to think about it. Yes. It's exactly what I deserve. "I don't need anything else."

The butler leaves the door open several inches when he goes. His departure stirs the air in the room, moving it over my skin and my tight nipples and between my legs. It whispers there while I wait for my husband to find me.

Chapter Thirteen

Francisco

An hour passes after I send up the annulment papers.

It's as long as I can bear. My patience seems to have abandoned me. I'm no longer sure that I made the right choice in restraining myself. Perhaps I should have let her see what I felt. Perhaps I should let her see what I feel now. I won't let her see everything. I won't let her see the cold fear that she has already signed the papers and left my house forever.

If she's going to do that, the least I can do is escort her to the door.

I told myself that I was not a man who would fall to his knees, not a man who would admit he'd fallen in love, not a man to beg his wife to stay. And it's true. I'm not that man, but maybe I can become him—for her. She's worth that and more.

Isabella is not in the ballroom, or any of the sitting rooms, or the library. She hasn't sought solace in the kitchen or the garden. Every place she is not seems strangely empty. It turns my stomach to think of her gone.

The last place I look is her bedroom.

The door's been left open. Not wide open, but open nonetheless. That's a reason for hope, isn't it? She hasn't tried to lock me out. I push the door open in one hand and go in.

Heat is the first thing to caress my face. Heat, because there's a fire going. And because Isabella is naked.

Bound on the bed. Her arms stretched wide. Her legs stretched wider. She's bound and helpless, and I can tell from the rise in her chest that she knows I'm here.

My cock is iron inside my pants, but the scene doesn't make sense. The fire in the hearth. Her naked body on the bed. "Hello, wife."

Her mouth works. "Hello, sir."

Hope is a hard drumbeat. "Sir, is it?" I keep my voice mild. Tone level. "What about the annulment?"

"The papers are over there." She tilts her head in the direction of the fireplace. My portfolio sits empty on one of the chairs. Isabella burned them. They are nothing but smoke and ash. I step to the grate to confirm it and turn off the flames. Then I go to the side of Isabella's bed, hands in my pockets to disguise their shaking. My wife looks up at me, eyes huge and glistening. "I don't want an annulment."

"So you've decided to stay."

I've never felt this nervous and hopeful and adrift before. I don't quite trust the sensation. It seems like the high before a crash. Before the world comes tumbling down around you and you're left with nothing.

Isabella's chin quivers. "I want nothing more in the world than to stay. If you'll let me."

"If I'll let you." The breath goes out of me. "I would have chased you out the door and dragged you back in. You are my wife. You are mine. Forget what I said and stay."

"Yes." The word from her lips feel more final than our wedding vows. A promise. "I will."

I don't bother with my clothes. I climb up onto the bed between my wife's spread legs and dip my head to the sweetness there. The moan that escapes her is filled with relief and desire and an apology, too. She has made her body one gorgeous apology. In return, I'll give her this.

I lick her from top to bottom while she lifts her hips to meet my face. I tease her folds and suck at her clit and use my teeth on the sensitive places that make her pant and writhe against her bonds. I fuck her hole with the tip of my tongue. I take her until she comes, and then I make her come again.

Isabella gasps when I leave the bed. "Don't go," she cries.

I laugh, the sound hoarse and unsteady. "I would never."

What I will do is strip off my clothes and release her from her prison. Back on the bed I take her in my hands and turn her so that she's on top, her thighs straining to keep herself positioned over me. "Can I?" she asks. "Please?"

"Take what you want."

Isabella lowers herself down onto my cock inch by inch. There's a regal quality to the way she moves as she handles the stretch and the invasion. She's so tight. So wet. Her muscles pulse, and it pulls a groan out of me that lights up her face. I keep my hands on her hips and guide her down until she's fully seated. Isabella rocks her hips back and forth, moaning so sweetly I don't know how I ever fought with her. I'll let her ride me. I'll let her be a queen in this house.

Her hands dig into my chest. My wife uses my cock with valiant passion, her pussy fluttering and gripping. But then her eyes open and fix on mine. Isabella leans down and kisses me, the tip of her tongue tentative on my lip. "I want—"

"Anything."

She shifts herself against me and pulls, turning us so that I'm braced over her. My wife throws her head back on the pillow and sighs. "Like this. I like it this way."

"On your back?"

"With you in charge." Her eyes meet mine with lust and seriousness. "I want you to be the one in charge. I want you to have control." She strokes my cheek with her fingertips. It's not a particularly erotic touch, but it makes my cock jump regardless. "You were right about my father."

"If you want to attend your meeting, then I'm sure it can be rearranged—"

"No. You were right," she insists. "He should handle his own business. I saved him once. I don't need to do it again. I belong with my husband now."

I bend my head to her collarbone and lick along the delicate curve. "Damn right you do."

Isabella's thighs are spread for me, drawing me in, and I push myself back inside her warmth with a stroke that makes her gasp. "Like this?"

"Almost," she breathes.

I make a collar of my hand on her throat. "What about this, my dear wife?"

She tips her head back another inch to find more contact. "Like that."

A gentle squeeze of my fingers, and her pussy clenches around my cock. She likes being restrained, she likes the hint of fear. She likes everything I have to give her. She really was made for me. I knew that early. What I didn't realize is that I was also made for her. My cock was made to fill her sweet pussy, my hands were made to pleasure her. My heart was made to beat for her, wanting more, needing it—a woman strong enough to stand up to me.

And a love deep enough to endure.

Epilogue

Isabella

"Thirty minutes."

My husband puts a hand on my arm and runs his palm down over bare skin. Down to my elbow. Down to my wrist, and my hand, where it rests on the railing of our baby's crib. "You can't abandon the dinner party after thirty minutes. Ninety, at least."

"Forty-five." Like most things in our life, it's a negotiation.

"You deserve more of a break than forty-five minutes." He pulls me close against him, and through the fabric of my dress I can feel the outlines of his tux.

One year after our wedding, and he still takes my breath away in black tie.

I only have eyes for our daughter in this moment. I know, I know. We can't spend all our time staring at a sleeping baby. But look at Francesca. She enjoyed the attention of our small house party all day, being oohed and ahhed over, but now it's time for her to rest.

And for us to enjoy a few hours of grown-up time.

Rare grown-up time, now that we have a baby.

Francisco turns me gently away from the crib. "Chessa won't be alone for a moment." He's right. The night nanny is waiting in the next room. And perhaps more importantly, Wolf has sentry duty lying beside her crib. "Come with me."

"I didn't know it would be this hard to leave her," I admit, blinking away the threat of tears. I've been emotional since I got pregnant. I thought it might ease once I gave birth, but I'm always on the brink of tears. "It's downstairs, not across the ocean."

"So much cuddling," he says, tsking as if he's a strict father. "We'll spoil her this way. She can be alone for an hour or two without us hovering over her."

In truth he's the one usually cuddling her, planting kisses on her warm forehead, showing her how to pet Wolf, changing her so that I can get a moment of sleep. He's the indulgent one between us, rocking her late into the night because she wants to be held.

But he's right, the way he usually is, so I give our sleeping baby one last kiss on her dark hair and take Francisco's offered arm.

"What's wrong?" he asks.

I haven't said anything. There's been no change in my expression, but he knows anyway. He's perceptive, my husband. And persistent, so I don't bother denying it. "I'm worried," I admit.

"About the dinner? Chef's taken care of everything."

In consultation with Frans, of course. Most people outside of our close circle of friends wouldn't know this, but he's actually quite comfortable managing our domestic affairs. I'm usually the one going over the financials, both personally and in our holdings. It's perhaps a little backwards to what some people expect, but it works for us.

"About us," I say, smoothing down my voluminous satin skirts. He's never stopped dressing me since our wedding, my husband. There are always new designer clothes and gowns to wear. Never boring black pantsuits. "I'm so happy. Too happy. What if it doesn't last?"

We're almost at the big double doors to the dining room. I can see our friends Liam and Samantha, leaning close to another couple for conversation. Frans introduced me to them when they stayed with us a few months ago, and now we're fast friends. Samantha is a professional violinist, and she's kind enough to play duets with me on the piano, even though I'm an amateur. And there's my friend Harper who I knew from my party days in New York City. She's all grown up, now, too, and married to the love of her life. I can already smell something incredible wafting from the kitchens. The guests have glasses of wine and champagne. The piano waits in the center of the small room, ready for whenever I want to wander over and play.

I'm putting on the smile I use for company when Francisco stops.

My husband takes my face in both his hands, careful not to disturb the makeup. He's exactly as beautiful as he was the first day I saw him, seated across the boardroom table. More beautiful. He'll never be a soft man, but his sharpest edges have been eased by intimacy. I know the love and devotion that burns beneath that hard expression.

"Stay as long as you want. Ten minutes or three hours. If you want to disappear upstairs to stare at our adorable creation, you can. Or bring her down here in a sling, if you want."

I grant him a small smile. "You're giving me permission because I'm anxious?"

"Because you are the smartest, strongest, most powerful woman I've ever known. You can do as you please. There is no one who can tell you what to do." A glint appears in his dark eyes. "Except when we're back in bed, tonight. Then you're mine to do with as I please."

My breathing speeds up. "And what about you? When will you be mine?"

He leans down to brush his lips against mine. "Do you need to ask, my dear wife? I already belong to you. I have since the first moment I saw you. Torture me. Please me. Do with me what you will, because I'm utterly, irrevocably yours."

* * * *

Also from 1001 Dark Nights and Skye Warren, discover The Bishop.

Sign up for the 1001 Dark Nights Newsletter
and be entered to win a Tiffany Key necklace.

There's a contest every month!

Go to www.1001DarkNights.com to subscribe.

**As a bonus, all subscribers can download
FIVE FREE exclusive books!**

Discover 1001 Dark Nights Collection Eight

DRAGON REVEALED by Donna Grant
A Dragon Kings Novella

CAPTURED IN INK by Carrie Ann Ryan
A Montgomery Ink: Boulder Novella

SECURING JANE by Susan Stoker
A SEAL of Protection: Legacy Series Novella

WILD WIND by Kristen Ashley
A Chaos Novella

DARE TO TEASE by Carly Phillips
A Dare Nation Novella

VAMPIRE by Rebecca Zanetti
A Dark Protectors/Rebels Novella

MAFIA KING by Rachel Van Dyken
A Mafia Royals Novella

THE GRAVEDIGGER'S SON by Darynda Jones
A Charley Davidson Novella

FINALE by Skye Warren
A North Security Novella

MEMORIES OF YOU by J. Kenner
A Stark Securities Novella

SLAYED BY DARKNESS by Alexandra Ivy
A Guardians of Eternity Novella

TREASURED by Lexi Blake
A Masters and Mercenaries Novella

THE DAREDEVIL by Dylan Allen
A Rivers Wilde Novella

BOND OF DESTINY by Larissa Ione
A Demonica Novella

THE CLOSE-UP by Kennedy Ryan
A Hollywood Renaissance Novella

MORE THAN POSSESS YOU by Shayla Black
A More Than Words Novella

HAUNTED HOUSE by Heather Graham
A Krewe of Hunters Novella

MAN FOR ME by Laurelin Paige
A Man In Charge Novella

THE RHYTHM METHOD by Kylie Scott
A Stage Dive Novella

JONAH BENNETT by Tijan
A Bennett Mafia Novella

CHANGE WITH ME by Kristen Proby
A With Me In Seattle Novella

THE DARKEST DESTINY by Gena Showalter
A Lords of the Underworld Novella

Also from Blue Box Press

THE LAST TIARA by M.J. Rose

THE CROWN OF GILDED BONES by Jennifer L. Armentrout
A Blood and Ash Novel

THE MISSING SISTER by Lucinda Riley

Discover More Skye Warren

The Bishop
A Tanglewood Novella

A million dollar chess piece goes missing hours before the auction.

Anders Sorenson will do anything to get it back. His family name and fortune rests on finding two inches of medieval ivory. Instead he finds an injured woman with terrible secrets.

He isn't letting her go until she helps him find the piece. But there's more at stake in this strategic game of lust and danger. When she confesses everything, he might lose more than his future. He might lose his heart.

Private Property
Rochester Trilogy Book 1
By Skye Warren

"This. Book. The characters. You will fall in love with them, and you will devour this book so quickly, you'll end up wanting to read it all over again. I loved it!"—*New York Times* bestselling author Monica Murphy

When I signed up for the nanny agency, I didn't expect a remote mansion on a windswept cliff. Or a brooding billionaire who resents his new role. His brother's death means he's now in charge of a moody seven year old girl. She's lashing out at the world, but I can handle her. I have to. I need the money to finish my college degree. As long as I can avoid the boss who alternately mocks me and coaxes me to reveal my darkest secrets.

"Skye Warren's modern, steamy retelling of Jane Eyre hooked me from page one! A moody, fast-paced and deliciously dirty read."—*New York Times* bestselling author Elle Kennedy

PRIVATE PROPERTY is a full-length contemporary novel from New York Times bestselling author Skye Warren about secrets and redemption. It's the first book in the emotional Rochester trilogy.

"An incredible five star read! Skye Warren delivers an unconventional, yet utterly explosive romance in Private Property."— *USA Today* bestselling author Jenika Snow

* * * *

I jump back as white lights blind me, moving in wild arcs across my body, across the building. It's a car. It's a car! And it's coming for me. I scream and back up against the wall as if it can somehow protect me from the careening vehicle.

Lights flash and flicker. The stone is freezing cold through my clothes.

And then stillness.

As suddenly as the headlights appeared, they stop moving.

I'm still pinned against the mansion like a butterfly in a frame, but at least I'm still alive. A car door slams, and then there's a large shadow looming over me.

"What the fuck are you doing? You could have been killed," says the shadow.

Somehow his voice booms over the rain, as if it's above ordinary things like the weather. I open my mouth to reply, but pinned butterflies can't speak. Everyone knows this. Shock holds my throat tight even as my heart pounds out of my chest.

"You don't belong here. This is private property."

I swallow hard. "I'm Jane Mendoza. The new nanny. Today is my first day."

There's silence from the shadow. In the stretching silence he turns into a man. A large one who seems impervious to the cold. "Jane," he says, testing my name. "Mendoza."

He says it with this northeastern accent I recognize from the Uber driver. Mend-ohhh-sah. In Texas, most people were used to Mexican last names. I'm wondering if that will be different in Maine. Maybe I would do a better job of defending myself if I weren't about to get hypothermia, if I hadn't just traveled two thousand miles for the first time in my life.

All I can hear are the words you don't belong here.

I've never belonged anywhere, but definitely not on this cliffside. "I work here. I'm telling the truth. You can ask inside. If we can get inside, I'm sure Mr. Rochester will tell you."

"He will."

I can't tell if it's disbelief in his tone. "Yes, he knows I'm coming. The Bassett Agency sent me. They told him I'm coming. He's probably waiting inside for me right now."

"No," he says. "I'm not."

My stomach sinks. "You're Mr. Rochester."

"Beau Rochester." He sounds grim. "I didn't get an email, but I haven't checked lately. I've been busy with… other things."

I fumble with my phone, which is incurably wet at this point. "I can show you. They sent my resume. And then the contract? Well, that's what they told me anyway—"

He's not listening. He turns around and circles back to the driver's side of the vehicle, which I can see now isn't a car, but is instead some kind of rough-terrain four-wheel thing. There are apparently no windows, only metal bars forming a crude frame. The kind of thing a rancher might use to move around his property or a good old boy might use for recreation.

I have no idea why this particular man has one, or is out using it tonight, until he turns off the lights. The engine goes quiet. He returns to me holding something small and shivering beneath his jacket. He shoves it into my freezing hands, and I fumble with my phone before pushing it into my jeans pocket.

"Here," he says. "You're good at taking care of things, right?"

There's a spark of fur covering tiny bones. It takes me a second of curling it close to my body to realize that it's a kitten. It mews, more movement than sound, its small mouth opening to show small white teeth. "Why do you have your kitten outside in the storm?"

"It's not mine. I saw it walking along the cliffs from my window when it started raining. Then it slipped and fell over the side. It took me this long to go down and search for him."

Shock roots me to the ground. "The kitten fell off a cliff?"

"Consider this your interview. You keep the small animal alive. You get the job."

About Skye Warren

Skye Warren is the New York Times bestselling author of dangerous romance. Her books have sold over one million copies. She makes her home in Texas with her loving family, sweet dogs, and evil cat.

For more information, visit https://www.skyewarren.com.

Discover 1001 Dark Nights

TRICKED by Rebecca Zanetti ~ DIRTY WICKED by Shayla Black ~ THE ONLY ONE by Lauren Blakely ~ SWEET SURRENDER by Liliana Hart

COLLECTION FOUR
ROCK CHICK REAWAKENING by Kristen Ashley ~ ADORING INK by Carrie Ann Ryan ~ SWEET RIVALRY by K. Bromberg ~ SHADE'S LADY by Joanna Wylde ~ RAZR by Larissa Ione ~ ARRANGED by Lexi Blake ~ TANGLED by Rebecca Zanetti ~ HOLD ME by J. Kenner ~ SOMEHOW, SOME WAY by Jennifer Probst ~ TOO CLOSE TO CALL by Tessa Bailey ~ HUNTED by Elisabeth Naughton ~ EYES ON YOU by Laura Kaye ~ BLADE by Alexandra Ivy/Laura Wright ~ DRAGON BURN by Donna Grant ~ TRIPPED OUT by Lorelei James ~ STUD FINDER by Lauren Blakely ~ MIDNIGHT UNLEASHED by Lara Adrian ~ HALLOW BE THE HAUNT by Heather Graham ~ DIRTY FILTHY FIX by Laurelin Paige ~ THE BED MATE by Kendall Ryan ~ NIGHT GAMES by CD Reiss ~ NO RESERVATIONS by Kristen Proby ~ DAWN OF SURRENDER by Liliana Hart

COLLECTION FIVE
BLAZE ERUPTING by Rebecca Zanetti ~ ROUGH RIDE by Kristen Ashley ~ HAWKYN by Larissa Ione ~ RIDE DIRTY by Laura Kaye ~ ROME'S CHANCE by Joanna Wylde ~ THE MARRIAGE ARRANGEMENT by Jennifer Probst ~ SURRENDER by Elisabeth Naughton ~ INKED NIGHTS by Carrie Ann Ryan ~ ENVY by Rachel Van Dyken ~ PROTECTED by Lexi Blake ~ THE PRINCE by Jennifer L. Armentrout ~ PLEASE ME by J. Kenner ~ WOUND TIGHT by Lorelei James ~ STRONG by Kylie Scott ~ DRAGON NIGHT by Donna Grant ~ TEMPTING BROOKE by Kristen Proby ~ HAUNTED BE THE HOLIDAYS by Heather Graham ~ CONTROL by K. Bromberg ~ HUNKY HEARTBREAKER by Kendall Ryan ~ THE DARKEST CAPTIVE by Gena Showalter

COLLECTION SIX
DRAGON CLAIMED by Donna Grant ~ ASHES TO INK by Carrie Ann Ryan ~ ENSNARED by Elisabeth Naughton ~ EVERMORE by Corinne Michaels ~ VENGEANCE by Rebecca Zanetti ~ ELI'S TRIUMPH by Joanna Wylde ~ CIPHER by Larissa Ione ~

RESCUING MACIE by Susan Stoker ~ ENCHANTED by Lexi Blake ~ TAKE THE BRIDE by Carly Phillips ~ INDULGE ME by J. Kenner ~ THE KING by Jennifer L. Armentrout ~ QUIET MAN by Kristen Ashley ~ ABANDON by Rachel Van Dyken ~ THE OPEN DOOR by Laurelin Paige ~ CLOSER by Kylie Scott ~ SOMETHING JUST LIKE THIS by Jennifer Probst ~ BLOOD NIGHT by Heather Graham ~ TWIST OF FATE by Jill Shalvis ~ MORE THAN PLEASURE YOU by Shayla Black ~ WONDER WITH ME by Kristen Proby ~ THE DARKEST ASSASSIN by Gena Showalter

COLLECTION SEVEN
THE BISHOP by Skye Warren ~ TAKEN WITH YOU by Carrie Ann Ryan ~ DRAGON LOST by Donna Grant ~ SEXY LOVE by Carly Phillips ~ PROVOKE by Rachel Van Dyken ~ RAFE by Sawyer Bennett ~ THE NAUGHTY PRINCESS by Claire Contreras ~ THE GRAVEYARD SHIFT by Darynda Jones ~ CHARMED by Lexi Blake ~ SACRIFICE OF DARKNESS by Alexandra Ivy ~ THE QUEEN by Jen Armentrout ~ BEGIN AGAIN by Jennifer Probst ~ VIXEN by Rebecca Zanetti ~ SLASH by Laurelin Paige ~ THE DEAD HEAT OF SUMMER by Heather Graham ~ WILD FIRE by Kristen Ashley ~ MORE THAN PROTECT YOU by Shayla Black ~ LOVE SONG by Kylie Scott ~ CHERISH ME by J. Kenner ~ SHINE WITH ME by Kristen Proby

Discover Blue Box Press
TAME ME by J. Kenner ~ TEMPT ME by J. Kenner ~ DAMIEN by J. Kenner ~ TEASE ME by J. Kenner ~ REAPER by Larissa Ione ~ THE SURRENDER GATE by Christopher Rice ~ SERVICING THE TARGET by Cherise Sinclair ~ THE LAKE OF LEARNING by Steve Berry and MJ Rose ~ THE MUSEUM OF MYSTERIES by Steve Berry and MJ Rose ~ TEASE ME by J. Kenner ~ FROM BLOOD AND ASH by Jennifer L. Armentrout ~ QUEEN MOVE by Kennedy Ryan ~ THE HOUSE OF LONG AGO by Steve Berry and MJ Rose ~ THE BUTTERFLY ROOM by Lucinda Riley ~ A KINGDOM OF FLESH AND FIRE by Jennifer L. Armentrout

On Behalf of 1001 Dark Nights,

Liz Berry, M.J. Rose, and Jillian Stein would like to thank ~

Steve Berry
Doug Scofield
Benjamin Stein
Kim Guidroz
Social Butterfly PR
Ashley Wells
Asha Hossain
Chris Graham
Chelle Olson
Kasi Alexander
Jessica Johns
Dylan Stockton
Richard Blake
and Simon Lipskar

Made in the USA
Las Vegas, NV
29 May 2021